A Candlelight Ecstasy Romance®

"WHY DID YOU TELL ME THOSE TERRIBLE LIES?" RHEA DEMANDED.

Hux saw the hurt in her eyes. "I did it to convince you that I was a sad and lonely man. And it worked, didn't it?" he said unhappily.

"You've made a fool of me too," she whispered. "Why did you do it, Hux?"

"I wasn't trying to make a fool of you, Rhea. I just wanted to . . . get closer to you."

"I can imagine how close you wanted to get!" She struggled free of his arms. "I should have known never to trust you!"

"Rhea, I was attracted to you and I got carried away trying to make you feel something for me. I'm sorry—"

"Don't bother apologizing," she said coldly. "I've seen you for the man you are—shallow, manipulative, heartless. I don't ever want to see you again!"

CANDLELIGHT ECSTASY ROMANCES®

JUST A LOT
MORE
TO LOVE

Lynn Patrick

A CANDLELIGHT ECSTASY ROMANCE®

Published by
Dell Publishing Co., Inc.
1 Dag Hammarskjold Plaza
New York, New York 10017

Dell ® TM 681510, Dell Publishing Co., Inc.

Candlelight Ecstasy Romance®, 1,203,540, is a registered
trademark of Dell Publishing Co., Inc.

ISBN: 0-440-14409-4

Printed in the United States of America

May 1986

10 9 8 7 6 5 4 3 2 1

WFH

*To the hidden beauty in
every woman—and to the men
who recognize it.*

To Our Readers:

We have been delighted with your enthusiastic response to Candlelight Ecstasy Romances®, and we thank you for the interest you have shown in this exciting series.

In the upcoming months we will continue to present the distinctive sensuous love stories you have come to expect only from Ecstasy. We look forward to bringing you many more books from your favorite authors, and also the very finest work from new authors of contemporary romantic fiction.

As always, we are striving to present the unique, absorbing love stories that you enjoy most—books that are more than ordinary romance. Your suggestions and comments are always welcome. Please write to us at the address below.

Sincerely,

The Editors
Candlelight Romances
1 Dag Hammarskjold Plaza
New York, New York 10017

JUST A LOT
MORE
TO LOVE

CHAPTER ONE

"Elegant . . . Dazzling . . . Electrifying! When the sun goes down, the fashions heat up. Turn on those night-lights—and the man of your choice—by wearing one of Ngamé's handpainted silks in shades of fuchsia, melon, turquoise, and marigold."

Intrigued by the fashion commentator's low throaty voice, Huxley Benton stopped just inside the doors of the Haldan-Northrop auditorium. Followed by individual spotlights, four turbaned models swayed down the ramp to Arabic music. He heard whispered murmurs as the gowns alternately clung to, then flowed around the pivoting models' lush hips and thighs.

Looking past them toward the podium, Hux could barely discern the outline of deep auburn curls tumbling over Rhea Mitchell's forehead. Her exquisite voice, however, amplified as it was by the loudspeakers, sent chills down his spine.

"Haldan-Northrop invites you to celebrate. The stars may be out tonight, but you'll be the one shining in Ngamé's beaded silver-silk chiffon. And when moonlight casts its midnight spell, don't resist. Revel in black magic."

Hearing the oohs and ahs from the audience, Hux reluctantly shifted his attention from Rhea to the two voluptuous women on stage. Men in the audience whistled. Ironic, but they probably wouldn't look twice if the models weren't garbed in Ngamé's glamorous clothing, he thought.

But what Hux wanted right now was to give Rhea Mitchell a second look. He'd met her once before because she'd represented Ngamé when the store decided to feature the new designer, and he vaguely remembered her as being attractive. As promotions director of Haldan-Northrop, Hux normally would have worked with Rhea on this fashion show. But he'd been preoccupied with the imminent opening of the Los Angeles branch of the Fifth Avenue store and had just spent a month in L.A.

He wasn't preoccupied now. Once more he was intrigued by the earthy sultriness of her voice, mixed with a natural warmth. Rhea Mitchell made Hux yearn for something he couldn't quite define—something that hadn't been a part of his past experiences in Manhattan's fast lane.

"Your man says he's too old to play with toys—but can he resist the temptation of hugging a soft teddy in luscious lavender? Mmm. And *naughty* can be oh-so-nice when French lace is lavished on marvelous magenta."

Rhea Mitchell was pleased by the audience's positive reaction to the glamorous and daring fashions modeled by striking women size fourteen and larger. And why not? One-fourth of all American women were considered "queen-sized." Smiling broadly, she introduced the new designer, who'd been her best

12

friend since they'd modeled together several years before.

"And now, the lady responsible for creating all this dazzling glamor for the queen-sized woman—Ngamé!"

A striking six-foot-tall black woman glided down the ramp, a handpainted African print clinging to her own ample curves. "I hope your enthusiasm is contagious," Ngamé said in a soft melodious voice, "so larger ladies everywhere can finally come out of the closet—looking lovely, that is!"

When the audience laughed, Rhea thought how fortunate she and her friend were. Each had found her own niche in the fashion world—Ngamé as a designer of glamorous clothing, Rhea as a fashion consultant with her own business.

The Hidden Woman was Rhea's pride and joy. As a teenager, she'd learned that appearances don't always reflect the inner person. Even then she'd thought of herself as more glamorous than her dress size indicated, so she'd learned to make her own clothing in self-defense. Ever since, she'd wished someone would champion the women who couldn't or wouldn't lose weight merely to conform. Now many of her customers were queen-sized, and with the help of designers like Ngamé, Rhea taught them to feel good about themselves in a "thin-is-in" world.

Suddenly the room lights went up and pandemonium broke loose. "Ngamé, I'd like to do a piece on you for the next issue of *B.P.!*" a reporter from *Beautiful People* magazine shouted.

"My camera crew can be backstage in five, Ngamé.

How about it?" asked the hostess of television's *Spot-light*.

"What do you think they'd say if I told them I'm really Martha Watson from Detroit?" Ngamé whispered to Rhea as she stepped off the stage. "Shall I reveal my humble beginnings?"

"Don't you dare spoil the illusion. Customers want to say they have a Ngamé original, not a Martha Watson."

"You're right. Besides, the truth isn't fun. I'll say I'm a deposed East African princess ousted from her country by usurpers."

"Just be sure to tell them all the same thing," Rhea admonished her friend with a grin.

"I'll think of a special story for the promotions director though."

"Huxley Benton's here?" Rhea looked for the suave man, who until now had been conspicuous by his absence.

"No doubt taking credit for his assistant's work," Ngamé said, heading for the reporters who were multiplying like eager rabbits.

Searching for him, Rhea spotted Hux in animated conversation with store executives and reporters. His dark tan set off his blond hair, intensified the green of his eyes, and brightened his white teeth. He was gorgeous but probably as superficial as his looks! Aghast at the judgment she'd just made, Rhea chided herself. She hated it when people judged others on appearances alone. Wasn't that the inspiration behind The Hidden Woman?

Just then Hux looked Rhea straight in the eye and aimed a very purposeful, slow, sexy smile her way.

The promotions director must have been sunning himself on some southern beach while everybody else was working his butt off planning the fashion show, she thought with irritation. And why was his smile aimed at her? Rhea gave the man a lukewarm smile, then deliberately walked into the crowd.

Hux ambled after Rhea Mitchell, intent on pursuing the sultry-voiced siren who'd seemed to snub him. Since he was stopped by at least a dozen media people, he made little progress across the room. For once, the fact that he knew everyone with connections in Manhattan irritated him.

Then he realized Rhea was greeting people as well, a warm, genuine smile curving her full lips. His heart thumped strangely when she threw back her head and laughed vivaciously at something a reporter from *The New York Times* whispered in her ear. She seemed vibrantly alive, with a glowing complexion and dark auburn hair smartly styled with a froth of curls tumbling over her forehead. She was a fascinating gypsy in bright teal and gold with jangling bracelets and earrings of pounded copper.

Knowing he was pretty much jaded when it came to beautiful women, Hux couldn't believe he was so intensely attracted to any woman, much less Rhea. The rational part of him argued she wasn't his type— he dated the sylphlike women he normally met in his profession. Intrigued and determined to find out whether his instincts and libido were overreacting, Hux quickly caught up to Rhea and greeted her with practiced savoir faire.

"Hello, darling," he said confidently, lightly kissing her on the cheek. "Good to see you again." Unabashed when Rhea stiffly drew back so he couldn't kiss the other cheek, he asked, "Looking for me?" and turned his most fail-proof smile on her.

Rich brown brows arched above large tilted amber eyes. How could he have looked into those exotic eyes before and not remembered them?

"Actually, I was looking for Ngamé," Rhea stated firmly.

"Oh? Well, soon the whole city will be looking for her—*at Haldan-Northrop.* We've really picked a winner. The sales on Ngamé's collection certainly will be worth all the time and money we've invested in her." Looking from Rhea to the reporter, Hux added, "Great show we put together, wasn't it?"

Rhea stared. What *we* was the man talking about? He'd certainly had no hand in promoting the fashion show. So Ngamé had been right. Mr. Gorgeous was anxious to take the credit.

"And the presentation was incredible. This lovely lady could sell me anything," Hux went on, slipping an arm over Rhea's shoulder and squeezing it familiarly. He added in a low husky tone, "With that sultry, seductive voice."

Annoyed, Rhea leaned into him, knocking him slightly off balance. "Why, thank you, Hux darling. You're lovely too." Savoring his startled expression, she moved a safe distance away. "Of course my presentation was aided by Ngamé's garments. They'll sell themselves."

"But her success at Haldan-Northrop will be the result of a joint effort—our contacts and Ngamé's brilliance," Hux insisted before turning his attention

16

to the reporter. "We think the right promotion will send this line over the top in a *big* way."

Big? Rhea silently echoed. Was Hux being subtly sarcastic about larger sizes?

"So you're prepared for success," the reporter said.

"The time has come to take women out of polyester pants," Hux replied. "I imagine many well-known designers will add a larger woman's line to their collections in the near future."

Rhea was irritated at the way Hux was taking over the conversation, as though he wanted the limelight for himself. Was that why he'd kissed her cheek and put an arm around her?

Of course the gestures were merely trappings of his social set—false friendships, empty embraces, nonsensical nicknames—all superficial. Rhea studied Hux critically as he droned on and on, talking about honing in on the pulse of the public to give it what it wants before the public knows what *it* is.

He was dressed in an outrageously expensive suit, sported a Porsche chronograph watch, and wore handmade Italian shoes that no doubt cost more than her entire designer outfit. He'd put most of the male models in *G.Q.* to shame, and make most women's mouths water. But Rhea wasn't most women. Hux was too sleekly good-looking, too wealthy, and undoubtedly too full of self-importance to interest her. He was exactly the type of man she generally avoided.

So why had she reacted so strongly when he'd put his arm on her shoulder?

Rhea realized she was the focus of Hux's attention when he remained after the reporter had gone.

"Can you really keep The Hidden Woman in business merely by staging fashion shows?" Hux asked.

"I also have individual clients," Rhea admitted. "I help them evaluate and revamp their wardrobes, hairstyles, and makeup to achieve the look they want, and to find the real women hidden inside of them."

"Queen-sized women?"

"Some are, although I don't discriminate. I'll take on anyone who wants me to discover her hidden beauty."

"*Your* beauty certainly isn't hidden," Hux murmured, staring at the hint of ample cleavage revealed by her silk blouse. "How would you like to discover *my* hidden beauty in return?"

Boldly looking him up and down, Rhea said, "I'd say some things about you are better left hidden, Huxley Benton."

Surprisingly, Hux laughed at that, his green eyes meeting hers in an odd kind of challenge.

"My job is to be known and make sure Haldan-Northrop gets known too," Hux told her. "Having all my secrets revealed is part of the deal."

"Yes, you are a professional," Rhea murmured in agreement, unable to stop herself from taking a pot-shot at him. "That tan looks professional too. What's your secret there? Did you buy it in the store's tanning salon?"

An expression of appreciation flickered over Hux's perfect features. "Actually I spent a few days in Puerto Vallarta after finishing business in L.A." Then he smiled that damned sexy smile again. "Since you're so curious about it, I'd be delighted to show you the rest of my tan."

"I hear Puerto Vallarta is one of the 'in' places to winter," she said, ignoring the blatant invitation. "You must keep up with the current trends." When he nodded, a suspicious gleam in his eyes, she examined his wide tie, turning it over to check the label. "It's hard work keeping up with what's in."

"But hard can be fun, *especially* when it's in."

Rhea felt herself blushing at that one. "But wouldn't it be nice to have your own personal style instead of following others?"

"You mean as in following your lead instead of someone else's? That might be interesting."

"I don't lead anyone. I merely try to help others discover and express their inner selves."

"Sounds to me like you're trying to drum up new clients. Tell you what," Hux said softly. "If you promise your consultations are very personal and extremely private, I'll consider hiring you."

"I don't usually cater to men, but I might make an exception in your case," Rhea said archly, running a finger along his jacket lapel. "If you really want to consult with me, we'll see if we can't find a real person underneath all that superficial gloss."

Something like hurt crossed Hux's face, but the vulnerable expression was quickly hidden by one much more cynical.

"Real people are hard to come by these days, aren't they?" he remarked. "But of course you wouldn't want it any other way since that's what keeps The Hidden Woman in business."

And she'd almost been ready to apologize to Mr.

Fast Talker Benton, Rhea thought indignantly. Then suddenly she realized she was enjoying herself even though Hux wasn't her type of man. Coming from a large garrulous family, which always seemed to be arguing—family discussion, her mother called it—Rhea was able to give Hux as good as she got. And she appreciated his quick repartee.

Rhea hadn't been the first one to comment on his glossy exterior, and it was a sore point with Hux. Not that he would ever admit it. . . . What would she say next? But before Rhea could make a comeback, they were interrupted by one of Haldan-Northrop's executive vice-presidents, a dynamic and attractive brunette.

"Rhea Mitchell, there you are. I've been looking for you," June Sterling said. "Hux, nice to see you." She was always the efficient executive, so Hux wasn't surprised that June didn't waste much time on pleasantries. She immediately got to the point. "Listen, Rhea, I've got a proposition for you."

"I already tried to proposition her, but she turned me down," Hux said in a stage whisper.

June laughed, wagged a warning finger at Hux, then immediately turned her attention back to Rhea. "I've been thinking about this deal since we met and I'm convinced it's a darned good idea. I've already tossed it into the pen, so to speak, and none of the old bulls has roared yet."

"What kind of deal?"

"I want The Hidden Woman for Haldan-Northrop. That kind of consulting service is exactly what we need."

"June, I don't know what to say. It took me three

20

years to build The Hidden Woman into a successful business. I can't just sell it."

"I don't want you to sell it. I'm talking about an exclusive contract with Haldan-Northrop. It'll still be your business, but you'll run it at the store. I know it'll increase our sales tremendously."

With Rhea's attention on her conversation with June, Hux couldn't help looking her over good and hard, tracing her full curves with hungry eyes. At first, he'd merely been intrigued by Rhea's sultry voice, but now there wasn't a part of her that didn't intrigue him.

"I plan to expand the concept of course, by adding a small boutique with glamorous garments for women of all sizes," June went on. "Today's success has convinced me that's essential."

"You're going a little fast for me. Honestly, the idea isn't really appealing . . ."

"Ah-ah!" June held up her hand. "No quick decisions. I'll call you in the morning to set up lunch. We can talk terms after you've had a chance to sleep on it." Without taking an extra breath, June Sterling was off, quickly disappearing into the surrounding throng.

"Is June always so forceful?" Rhea asked with a chuckle, still staring at the spot in the crowd where the vice-president had vanished.

The low timbre of her voice heated his insides, and Hux swallowed hard, forcing himself to answer casually. "June has what it takes, all right. I'll lay odds that she'll make chairman of the board within the next five years. Now, what was it you were about to say before our dynamic vice-president struck?" Hux prompted her, moving closer.

"I'm not sure I was going to say anything." Seeming flustered suddenly, Rhea checked her watch. "I've got to find Ngamé before I leave."

"Why don't you let me take you home? Better yet, we could go out for a drink and continue our conversation. Given time, I'm sure you'll recover your memory." Seeing she wasn't convinced, he added, "I can promise you a stimulating evening."

"Thanks, but I've had enough stimulation for one day," Rhea said, making a remarkable recovery. "I never do anything in excess. It's not good for the health."

"That's what I like about you, Rhea Mitchell. You're never at a loss for words. I appreciate a witty woman."

He thought he almost had her then. He saw indecision reflected in her amber eyes. But then it was gone. "You'll have to be appreciative without me then. Good-bye, Huxley Benton."

"It's not good-bye," Hux called after her retreating form, and was rewarded when she flashed a quick smile over her shoulder.

"C'mon, Hux, old man, pay attention to your friends here," a reporter said behind the promotions director, Hux following Rhea's gently swaying hips. "She's not exactly your type."

"Hux doesn't have a type," another insisted. "He likes anything in skirts—or without them. Haven't you seen his string of beauties?"

"But he probably could fit two of them into this one's skirt," the first said with a snicker.

22

"You've been hanging around with Leticia too long, Gary," Hux told his friend, referring to a spiteful gossip columnist who wrote for the same newspaper. "I'm worried you might meow."

Hux stalked off, tempted to punch the man. Gary didn't know a thing about Rhea. Nor had he been interested. He'd only judged her by superficial standards. And he'd judged wrong.

Tall and broad-shouldered, Rhea was well-proportioned with full breasts and hips, her narrower waist accentuated by a copper belt that matched her gypsy jewelry. She'd seemed lush and beautiful to him.

He then visualized one of the actresses he'd dated recently, and remembered how she'd felt kind of bony in his arms. He'd bet Rhea Mitchell would feel soft and plush—a real *woman* in comparison!

He couldn't wait.

Then Hux realized that for once his charm hadn't worked on a woman. Rhea hadn't fallen for his line. It was part of her charm, but it also meant he'd have to find another way of getting to her. Savoring the unique taste of the chase, Hux scanned the room until he spotted June Sterling.

Smiling broadly, he approached the vice-president. Perhaps she'd be able to help him flush out the hidden woman he wanted to know better.

CHAPTER TWO

"Yes, Hux, we're delighted with your suggestions. The series of presentations by popular interior designers will be the best lead-in for our new Eurostyle approach," droned the woman who was the manager in charge of household products and home furnishings at Haldan-Northrop.

Barely listening, Hux managed to answer. "You can count on me to start working on those presentations right away." Smiling, he tried to hide his indifference from his companion as they took the elevator up to the store's business offices. Part of his job was to foster promotional enthusiasm and it wasn't anyone's fault he'd felt particularly unenthusiastic lately.

Taking leave of the woman at the end of their elevator ride, Hux looked over the busy staff at work. Without much interest he wondered what was on his agenda for the afternoon. He knew he should report directly back to his secretary to check the schedule. Instead he wandered over to the coffee machine and poured a cup.

"Been to lunch? Beautiful day out there," remarked a man passing by. "Warm for January."

"Yeah," Hux answered noncommittally, sipping his coffee.

This apathetic attitude was definitely unlike him. What was wrong? It was too soon for him to be bored with his job. Haldan-Northrop had opened only two years ago. And before taking this particular position, he'd always worked in the promotions field anyway. Hanging out with a stylish crowd in New York, Hux found the profession perfectly suited to a man into a trendy life-style.

So what was wrong? Was it time for some new incentive? Should he try to rise in the store's corporate hierarchy? Hux knew the vice-president in charge of promotions, advertising, and public relations was considering a lucrative job offer from Bloomingdale's.

Perhaps it wasn't the job. Walking toward his office, Hux speculated the problem might be more personal. He had to admit he wasn't happy with his social life lately. The freewheeling singles' scene he was expected to frequent—dinner and various entertainments almost every night, a different girl friend every few months—was beginning to wear on him. Wouldn't it be better to find someone caring and special, then date her steadily?

Hux felt a pang of regret, remembering his last liaison. The woman he'd been seeing, a self-centered model, had been more interested in making contacts with his acquaintances than in being with him. He hadn't heard from her since he'd introduced her to a well-known photographer a few weeks ago. And unfortunately for Hux, that sort of behavior by girlfriends was nothing unusual.

It was difficult to find a woman with no ulterior motives in Hux's crowd. Perhaps he should look for some new friends. If he wanted to make a change, however, he'd better do it soon, he cautioned himself. At thirty-eight he wasn't getting any younger. Suddenly worried about his age, Hux sneaked furtive looks at the mirrored walls between the elevators as he passed by.

"Any messages for me?" Hux asked, stopping beside his secretary's desk.

The young woman looked up at him nervously. *"She's* in there," she whispered, pointing at his office, "and she seems to be angry."

"Who's angry?" he said, lowering his voice.

"Rhea Mitchell," the secretary hissed back.

"Rhea?"

"She doesn't have an appointment!"

"That's all right. I want to talk to her anyway."

Hux was a little surprised. He knew he'd be hearing from Rhea shortly, but he didn't expect to see her in person. Feeling gathering excitement, he adjusted his tie and thought about the presumptuous—and totally inaccurate—message he'd left on Rhea's answering machine that morning. He'd told her he was launching some elaborate promotion plans for The Hidden Woman, and hadn't asked for her approval. No wonder she was angry! June Sterling had told him Rhea had agreed to merge her business with the store, but only if she retained her independence.

Of course, in reality, Hux had no intentions of launching anything. The message had only been a ploy. Since Rhea didn't seem interested in him on a personal level, he'd been forced to use business to get

26

her attention. Now that he'd succeeded in this first step, he'd have to find a way to transform her anger into romantic interest. Savoring the rush of adrenaline through his veins, he strode confidently into the office.

Sitting in a chrome-and-leather chair, Rhea glanced up as he entered, a slight frown creasing her smooth brow. Even so, Hux thought, the woman's full curving lips always looked like they were ready to smile. The light from the window set her auburn hair afire and, combined with the subtle peach of her sweater-dress, made her perfect skin appear to be lit from within.

"How nice to see you, Rhea," Hux told her, smiling broadly. "What can I do for you? Something personal, I hope."

She deliberately chose to ignore his flirtatious tone. "I got your phone message and decided we should talk immediately."

"How flattering." Placing his coffee cup on the desk, Hux walked over to take a seat in the chair next to hers.

"Don't be flattered," Rhea said. "I wasn't at all happy to hear your message."

"Really? What was wrong with it? Should I have used poetry? Perhaps sounded a little more amorous?" Trying to be nonchalant, Hux draped one of his arms over the chair's back and crossed his long legs. His foot, clad in Italian leather, nudged one of Rhea's low snakeskin pumps. He noticed she quietly moved her foot away.

"This doesn't have a thing to do with being amorous and you know it. I'm not happy with the fact that you're planning to send out flyers promoting The Hidden Woman and . . ."

"Don't worry. You can trust me to see that the flyers will be attractive."

"That's not the point. I'm not ready to have any flyers mailed out now. I decided to join Haldan-Northrop barely a week ago."

Large amber eyes intent, she regarded him closely. Hux cautioned himself to keep a straight face. He decided the peachy color she wore was incredibly erotic, reminding him of a luscious fruit. Was Rhea ripe for the picking?

"I'm not ready to think about promotions or advertising at the moment. And I don't see why it's necessary. The boutique won't open and my services won't be available there for a couple of months," she told him. "Furthermore . . ."

Pretending he didn't know what she was getting at, Hux interrupted her. "So I should just get all the flyers printed, stack them up, and wait for your signal? How are you going to let me know—*when you're ready?*" He emphasized the last phrase meaningfully.

"The same way I'm letting you know I'm *not* ready now."

"Great! Could you visit me at home next time— and wear something even slinkier? I like that color on you, by the way."

Rhea drew back as Hux leaned toward her. The subtle drift of his cologne almost made her dizzy. Was this man for real? Or did the promotions director routinely use his considerable charm to bamboozle female personnel and get his way? Surely it had to be the latter, because she'd already determined she wasn't Hux's type.

Not that he was as bad as she'd originally thought. From store personnel she'd talked with, she'd learned Hux was a thoughtful, even kindly boss. Unfortunately his treatment of employees had nothing to do with his treatment of women—Rhea had heard he'd had so many girl friends in the past year, his observers had lost track of them. He obviously regarded love affairs as conquests. It irritated Rhea that she found herself attracted to the man—certainly she could never take his flirting seriously. She'd have to continue to resist him. She didn't want to be dropped like his other women when he grew tired of her.

"Let's get this straight," Rhea said emphatically. "Forget about the flyers. I don't want them printed up until I write the copy for them. I'm the expert on my own business."

"What do you want to say?"

"I'm not sure yet."

"Well, it can't be that difficult. We'll want to include a description of your background and the kind of services you offer, along with a sexy photo of you."

"That's close, but not quite good enough, Hux. I prefer a more personalized approach. I want to address the customer and tell her what The Hidden Woman can really do for her. And with a personal quote I'll include a picture of me in one of Ngamé's garments."

"Hmm. One with a low-cut neckline, your head tossed back and your beautiful lips parted enticingly," Hux said, narrowing his bright green eyes and raking them over her as if he were imagining—and thoroughly enjoying—the shot.

Fighting to repress the unbidden thrill of arousal at his glance, Rhea argued, "The object of this flyer is to obtain customers for consultation, not lovers."

"But these women will want to appear sexy. That's why they'll decide to come to you."

"They'll want to be all kinds of things—sexy, successful, adventurous."

"But sex appeal is what sells in advertising."

Rhea wondered why she enjoyed arguing with Hux. He was a consummate double-talker, able to sound romantic at the same time as he discussed business. She'd be far better off leaving his office now and writing a carefully worded letter to the scoundrel. But she was in too deep, his verbal game was too stimulating, and his innuendos were so witty, she simply had to continue. Hadn't she come into his office angry, and wasn't she now half amused? At least she could take the time to show him the wit he'd professed to admire.

Rhea suggested, "If you want sex appeal, why don't we put a good-looking man in the photo with me, succumbing to my amazing charms."

Hux paused only a moment. "Hmm. Why don't we put a line of men in the photograph, all dressed in tuxedos and waiting to dance with you?"

The corners of her mouth twitching, Rhea decided to go another one up. "That sounds good, but I'm worried it might be a little static. I actually could be dancing with a group of men, but under a strobe light in a disco setting."

"A disco scene is outdated," Hux said decisively,

eyes alight with mischief. "We need to be more imaginative. Fantasy scenes are in now. Why don't we pose you on a seashell and then superimpose that photo onto an ocean background? The admiring men can be a crowd of surfers riding the swells, following you across the water."

"Like the goddess Venus rising from the sea?" asked Rhea, hoping her smile wouldn't give her away. She didn't want him to know she thought his silly idea amusing. So Hux wanted to be totally outrageous, huh? "If we're going to get mythological, why don't we have me pose as Helen of Troy? Then we can have the entire army of ancient Greece panting for my favors."

Hux considered the suggestion. Had he run out of ideas? Had she finally topped him? Preparing to accept victory graciously, Rhea watched him scratch his chin and narrow his eyes.

"Yes, that's good," he admitted. "But we have to appeal to current sensibilities. Some people don't know much about ancient Greece. It might be more effective to pose you as a glamorous, outer-space siren flying your vehicle around the moon with vast numbers of astronauts trying to catch up with you in rocket ships."

Picturing herself in a rhinestone-encrusted helmet and low-cut spacesuit, Rhea exclaimed, "Enough!" Then she erupted into peals of laughter. "I give up. Please stop," she gasped, "before we continue out into the solar system and the distant galaxies, encountering hosts of men more numerous than I can imagine!"

31

"Then you want to stick with the moon and astronaut idea?" he asked soberly.

She made a conscious attempt to pull herself together. "This is unbelievable," she complained. "I came here to tell you that you can't make promotion plans without consulting me. I end up debating ridiculous publicity shots."

"Ridiculous? Well, you're the one who began making ridiculous suggestions. I simply improved on your line of thinking."

"Improved my thinking?" Now Rhea was getting angry again. "You think my ideas are ridiculous? You're the one who exaggerated my original suggestions, Mr. Huxley Benton. I was just carrying things further to show you how ludicrous *your* ideas are."

"I would never be ridiculous or ludicrous unless I thought that's what you wanted. After all, I'm the store's promotions director and . . ."

"If you cared about doing what I wanted," Rhea interrupted, "you wouldn't make plans for promoting The Hidden Woman without consulting me. For your information, I have executive permission to have approval on anything that concerns my consulting service. I wouldn't have agreed to work here otherwise."

"So? I don't dispute that. I know about your agreement with June."

"Well, then why did you call me and say you were going to launch a mailing campaign and arrange for me to appear on television, which I won't do. Why did you do that without consulting me?"

"I *am* consulting you. What do you think we're doing here?"

"What? In your phone message you said you had already started to do these things."

"Perhaps it was my wording. I'm used to talking with a positive thrust."

"I'll just bet you are!" Rhea said, realizing he was turning the conversation with sexy double entendres again.

Would she be flattered if he told her the truth? He aimed what he hoped was a winning smile in her direction. "Ahem. I, uh, also had an ulterior motive. I wanted to see you again. I thought we could get together tonight for dinner and discuss future plans. Nothing wrong with mixing business and pleasure."

"I already have a dinner date."

"Well, can't you break it?"

Her amber eyes hardened. "No, I can't. I don't play games like that with my friends. Your ideas are not the only thing I find unbelievable, Hux. Do you actually think I'm going to be impressed because you left me a facetious telephone message just so you could get me down here and ask me for a date? That's professionally unethical."

"You didn't have to come down here," Hux objected, displeased the conversation wasn't going in the right direction. "You could have called me back instead. But now that you're here, why waste the trip?"

"I'm sure you knew I was going to react negatively when I got your message. Now I'm finding it hard to believe anything you say."

"That's why I think we should go out to dinner," Hux continued, unabashed by her accusation. "I may have made a mistake and we need to clear up the

33

matter. If not tonight, how about tomorrow? We have a lot of things to discuss."

"You don't give up, do you?"

"I'm very persistent."

"And competitive."

"I want to see you. What's wrong with that?"

Rhea stood, gathering up the wrap she'd thrown over the back of the chair. Getting to his feet as well, Hux helped drape the garment over her shoulders. Feeling the warm flesh beneath her clothing, his fingers lingered a little longer than necessary.

"Look, Hux," Rhea said, turning to face him. "I don't know why you're doing all of this, but I can see you like to play games. Maybe you're trying to impress me or compete with me or pull one over on me. I don't know."

"Why can't you just accept the fact that I'm attracted to you and am trying my best to get you to go out to dinner with me?"

"You must realize we aren't each other's type, Hux. Must you command every living, breathing woman's attention? Are you always looking for the chance to make a conquest?" She paused. "I think you're very attractive. There, I've said it. If you were a different kind of person, I wouldn't hesitate to go out with you. Isn't that good enough for you?"

The woman was damnably confusing. Scowling, Hux said, "You're still refusing to see me? What do you mean by saying we're not each other's type? Does that remark have anything to do with your opinionated reference to my not being a 'real' person? You're very judgmental, Rhea."

But she was already walking toward the door. He

followed closely, already trying to come up with another plan. Was she simply playing hard to get? Well, he'd participated in that game before and won.

"Rhea," he said. "Don't go away angry. We're going to have to work closely together soon."

"I'm not angry," she retorted, stopping on the other side of the secretary's desk. "And I'll see you in a couple of weeks—when June calls a meeting. I have to leave now to meet someone."

Irritated at feeling something close to jealousy, Hux wondered if Rhea were going off to meet a man —some unappreciative dolt she preferred over him. Walking around the desk to get closer, he almost trampled a tiny blonde waiting there. Only her stature could have made him overlook her, because she was dressed in a gauzy white fairy costume, complete with wings.

"Melissa!" Hux exclaimed in surprise.

Gazing up at him with clear blue eyes, Melissa spoke in a soft voice. "Hux, we had an appointment at three. I didn't want to interrupt your other meeting, but we need to talk. We have to decide when I'm going to leave the toy department and how to change my costume until I do leave."

She pointed to the material stretched tightly around her waist. "I can still do my story-telling fairy act, but I'm five months along, you know."

Hux found himself literally staring at Melissa's abdomen—and blushing. Cursing the incriminating warmth spreading across his face, he quickly tried to regain his self-control. Damn! Rhea was still standing there watching! For once, when he wanted it least, he'd gotten her undivided interest.

35

He gingerly placed a hand on the fairy's arm. "Here, um, why don't you come into my office? You'll be more comfortable sitting down, won't you? In your condition you shouldn't stand."

Melissa laughed with a tinkling sound appropriate only to a person of her appearance and stature. "Relax, Hux," she assured him as he led her inside and lowered her into a chair. "Don't worry. I'm not made of glass. I've been thinking I could simply raise the waistline of this dress and make it Empire style to hide my stomach. That should do for another month."

Standing up again, Melissa raised the dress at the waistline to show him. "See? We'll need to adjust my wings. Do you think this looks okay or should I quit the job right away?"

"Uh . . ." Hux felt himself blushing again as he gazed down at her. "Don't quit. We'll work out something. Now why don't we get a pillow to put under you before we talk?" He glanced through the doorway. Rhea had moved closer to get a better view.

She wasn't alone. A couple of file clerks and Hux's secretary had now joined her to avidly watch the goings-on. Glaring at the group as he moved to shut the door, Hux complained loudly, "I wonder why everything is so quiet this afternoon? I guess I'll have to come up with thousands of pages of typing and filing so the clerical staff won't be bored. In the meantime I'm going to close my door for some privacy."

Hearing low chuckles and murmurs from the women around her, Rhea reflected on what she'd just seen. She'd hardly been able to believe her eyes. Had

36

that really been the suave Huxley Benton who'd blushed so awkwardly? Who'd been so openly solicitous? Was the little fairy princess . . . a mistake of his? she wondered irritably.

Rhea wasn't the only one pondering the situation. One of the clerks broke into her train of thought by saying "Wow! What's going on? Has Hux gotten himself into hot water?"

Hux's secretary responded. "It's not what you think, Millie. That little woman is Melissa Damon. She works as the story-telling fairy down on the sixth floor and is married to Rafe Damon, a well-known child photographer. He and Hux are good friends."

"Is that all?" asked the clerk. "Darn! I thought we were witnessing a juicy scene. Wasn't it fun to watch Mr. Sophisticated get all flustered and uncomfortable?"

The other clerk laughed and said, "He'd be more embarrassed if he knew what you were honestly thinking! And he was mad as heck anyway. I wonder if he'll really give us a ton of filing to do."

"Don't worry," Hux's secretary advised them. "Hux's bark is worse than his bite. We'd better get back to work though."

Beaming at the women as they dispersed, Rhea headed toward the elevators with a springy step and a wide grin on her face. Then, aware of what she was doing, she intentionally slowed down. She needn't be so delighted at witnessing the sight of Huxley Benton displaying his more vulnerable human side. That shouldn't matter to her in the least. They were business associates—that was all. And she knew she had better keep it that way.

CHAPTER THREE

"I hope I'm going to like it here and that I haven't made a mistake," said Rhea as she surveyed the space for her new boutique and office on the store's designer clothing floor. It was empty now except for several workmen and huge piles of discarded boards and plaster.

"Don't be so negative," said Ngamé, her bracelets jangling as she brushed some powdery plaster off her bright-magenta coat. "Aren't you going to make more money now? And can't you pull out later if you want to? What did they say in that important meeting this morning?"

They'd met for lunch after Rhea had attended June Sterling's meeting. Now the two of them were curiously prowling the designated area.

"June assured me—once again—that I can be semi-independent."

"So you've got no problems, girl," said Ngamé.

"Not yet."

"Trouble's going to find you if you go looking for it. You need something to take your mind off all these changes. Know any sexy men?"

Rhea laughed. "I haven't had much time for men lately."

"Well, what about that handsome promotions director? He sure seemed to be giving you the eye at the fashion show. What's his name? Huntley? Humphrey?"

"Huxley Benton," Rhea said. "He was at the meeting this morning and I have to drop by and talk to him about promotion this afternoon."

"Is that why you wore your favorite purple dress today?"

"No. Put the idea of any romance with Hux out of your mind."

"Why? Is he married?"

"He's a playboy who likes to parade fashion models around on his arm."

"Well, maybe he's ready for someone different."

Rhea was tempted to tell Ngamé about the last encounter she'd had with Hux a couple of weeks ago. But her friend would think she was crazy if she knew the man had asked Rhea out and she'd refused.

"Hux is not my type," Rhea stated. "He's too fashionable and trendy and I'd rather not talk about him."

But Ngamé was not to be put off. "Me oh my. Aren't we defensive. You sound very prejudicial, if you ask me. What have you got against him, honey? His good looks?"

Giving Ngamé a derisive glance, Rhea changed the subject. "By the way, I like your bracelets. I noticed them at lunch. Where did you get them?"

"These things?" Ngamé held up her wrists. "Aren't

they pretty? These are genuine goat bells—from Morocco."

"Hmm. Nice, if a little noisy."

"I always like to get my share of attention."

"You sure do," Rhea said, thinking Ngamé would be noticeable anywhere because of her height and unusual taste in clothes.

"Well, George really likes the sound of these bells." Ngamé referred to her longtime boyfriend. "He calls them love chimes. And speaking of love, what about that Humphrey Betton?"

"Huxley Benton. There's nothing more to say."

To Rhea's relief, Ngamé let the subject drop.

But looking over the space that would become The Hidden Woman's reception area and discussing furniture, Rhea couldn't get him out of her mind. He'd been so polite at this morning's meeting, she'd hardly recognized him as the argumentative man she'd met before. Thinking about how persistent he'd been back then and how attracted she still was, Rhea wondered if perhaps Ngamé was right about needing a new man in her life. If he asked her again, should she give Huxley Benton a whirl?

"Rhea!"

Recognizing a familiar voice, she half-expected to see the man of her thoughts. But it wasn't Hux who came walking across the rubble toward Rhea and Ngamé. Wearing a rather rumpled jacket, a shaggy haircut, and a worried look on his face, this man was hardly an example of classy male fashion.

"Jerry!" Rhea said, giving him a friendly hug. "It's good to see you." She and Jerry Hastings had dated in high school more than fifteen years ago, and were still good friends. "This is my friend Ngamé, the designer."

"Hi. Uh, I hope you don't mind my coming here."

"No. What's wrong?" Rhea asked, noting his expression.

Sweet and sensitive, Jerry was a little helpless in practical matters. And he'd been having a hard time lately. In the past year Jerry had suffered through a divorce and a death in the family, and had severe financial problems besides.

"Actually, nothing has changed radically since the last time I talked to you," he said, adjusting his crooked glasses. "I haven't sold any more novels because there's a glut in the Western market. Barbara is suing me for alimony. My co-op's falling apart."

"Sounds like you two need privacy," Ngamé said. "See you Saturday, Rhea."

Rhea watched the black woman walk toward the bank of escalators, and was startled when Ngamé stopped to talk to none other than Huxley Benton. Wanting to turn and stare, Rhea forced herself to ignore them and pay attention to Jerry.

"Actually, I called your sister this morning to find out where you'd be," Jerry admitted. "I didn't want to leave a message on your answering machine."

The workmen began tearing down some plasterboard and the noise got on Rhea's nerves. She motioned her old friend to follow her across the littered floor. Glancing to the escalators, she noticed both Ngamé and Hux had disappeared.

"To tell you the truth, Rhea, I do have a problem, and only you can help me."

41

"You know I'll do whatever I can to help," Rhea said gently. "Do you need a loan?"

He smiled at her, his cheeks slightly pink. "Oh, it has nothing to do with that, I assure you. Actually, the problem is tailoring."

"Tailoring?" Rhea stopped short.

"I know you're an expert and I can't afford to hire someone." Jerry seemed embarrassed and uncomfortable. "Do you think you might have the time to do me a big favor?"

"What do you need?"

"Well, I have a chance at an editorial job that could help me out financially."

"Wonderful!" She squeezed his arm.

"The only problem is I've got to go in for an interview and I've only got one decent-looking suit. I've lost so much weight the past year, it doesn't fit anymore. Even belted tightly, the pants almost fall off."

"I can loan you money for a new one."

"No, no." He raised his hands in objection. "I don't want to take any more money from you, and I don't want a new suit. I'd like my old one altered. I could pay you for the work when I get on my feet."

Rhea was so happy for Jerry, she decided she'd make time in her schedule to help him. "Nonsense," she said. "I won't accept your money. I'll come over to pin the suit on you and then I'll take it home to sew." She mentally made a list of things she'd need—pins, scissors, a seam ripper, tailor's chalk. "Hmm . . . I don't have any evenings available for a while. How about Saturday afternoon?"

"Then you can do it?" Jerry's face glowed with pleasure.

"Sure."

Aware of nearby movement, Rhea hoped the construction workers weren't listening to their conversation. Jerry would be so embarrassed. She was about to check for herself when her friend spoke in a lowered voice.

"Uh, the zipper of the pants is messed up too. It's stuck."

Forgetting the construction workers, Rhea grinned. "You've got another serious problem, huh?"

"Yeah, I can't get it to work anymore."

Peeking through a crack in a plasterboard panel. Hux held his breath as Rhea's eyes darted toward his hiding place. When she turned back to her companion, he exhaled in relief. He didn't want her to catch him eavesdropping.

"That can't be a very difficult problem, Jerry," said Rhea. "Have you tried taking a firm hold and really pulling on it?"

"Once, but I'm afraid I'll break something. I'm rather inept at these things."

"Well, I'm sure it will be okay. On Saturday I'll apply my advanced expertise."

"With your magic fingers, Rhea, everything is possible," said Jerry. "I really appreciate your services and I promise it's the last time. I don't want you to feel used."

Startled, Hux almost stumbled against the plasterboard panel. Good Lord, were they actually discussing the man's sexual problem? No wonder the poor guy looked so embarrassed.

"Don't worry about using me. I'll get a lot of plea-

43

sure out of helping a friend. I've been so busy building my business, I haven't had time for that kind of fun."

Hux couldn't believe his ears. Rhea was actually willing to help the guy out! Getting angry, Hux was about to tell the guy to get lost, but Rhea went on.

"Altering your old suit will be an easy task for me, and I'm sure I can repair the zipper of the pants also."

Startled once again, Hux tightly gripped the edge of the panel. They were talking about altering a suit! he realized with relief, then with pleasure.

"Say, how would you like me to fix you a gourmet lunch on Saturday?" asked Jerry.

"You don't have to do that. You can treat me when you get the new job." Rhea embraced him. "I've had some rough times myself. But everything will be fine, Jerry, I promise. You'll be able to wear the suit to the interview and look great. I'm sure I can fit you perfectly."

"I'd really like to do something for you, but I guess we can postpone the fancy feast for a while. You don't know how much this means to me. If I get that job, I'll be able to live normally again."

Rhea smiled at him warmly. "I'm happy I can help you out."

Then Jerry looked at his watch nervously. "Well, I've taken up enough of your time. See you Saturday afternoon." He started to leave but turned to add, "If you ever decide you want to be more than friends, I'll marry you on the spot!"

Jerry headed for the escalator, and then Hux saw Rhea check her watch. It was a little after four and she was late for their meeting in his office. As she walked toward the elevators, Hux carefully sneaked out from his hiding place and followed her. Halfway across the floor he caught up, ignoring her surprised expression.

"Rhea. I decided to see what was keeping you."

"Sorry. Have you been waiting? I was talking to an old friend."

"I noticed."

"Poor Jerry." Rhea sighed. "His wife left him last year and he hasn't been the same man since."

Hux couldn't help but grin widely, remembering how he'd first interpreted their seemingly X-rated conversation. "Problems, huh?"

She gazed at him curiously. "You can say that again. But if everything works out, by this time next week he'll have a new lease on life."

"Quite a few of us could use one of those," Hux said wryly, pulling out a handkerchief to wipe some powdery white dust from his hands.

She frowned. "Where did you get that plaster dust? Were you eavesdropping?"

"No, of course not," Hux denied. "There's plaster flying all around here. I have to admit, though, I did overhear you say something about helping that guy with his sewing." Her narrowed eyes made him squirm. He wondered if she'd question him further.

"Anyway," he went on brusquely, trying to appear nonchalant, "another reason I came down here was to ask if you'd like to talk business over a drink. Going out will be far more pleasant than meeting in my office. The entire floor upstairs is torn up by the new phone lines we're putting in."

"Sure," Rhea agreed, her expression suddenly softening. "I'd enjoy a drink."

As they left Haldan-Northrop and walked to a popular bar nearby, Hux let Rhea do most of the talking. He thought about how sweet and supportive she could be. Not many people would have volunteered time and skill to help a friend get a job. As far as he could see, she'd had no selfish, ulterior motives. Why couldn't Hux have someone like Rhea in his life?

Of course he wanted her for much more than sewing. Unlike Jerry, Hux was not willing to be only Rhea's friend. Since she seemed immune to his practiced charm and the schemes he'd tried so far, he'd have to come up with a new and better approach.

Hux was still wracking his brains about that problem when they arrived at the pub. During the first drink he and Rhea talked about general promotion needs for the upcoming boutique. With the second drink and appetizers they noticed the music video playing on the pub's television set. Then they were both enthusiastically discussing the possibility of doing a fashion video for The Hidden Woman. Several New York designers had already made fashion videos to promote their garments. It was the first thing they'd agreed on, Hux thought with satisfaction.

"I'll start working on a story line right away," said Rhea excitedly as she sipped her margarita. "I can picture everything. What a way to turn the public on to The Hidden Woman."

Admiring the lively sparkle in her eyes and the expanse of peachy skin revealed by the low vee of her purple dress, Hux was turned on by thoughts of

46

other things. But he said, "It's a good idea all right. I'll be working closely with you, of course."

"Of course. That's part of your job."

"Then we'd better start as soon as possible. Why not meet this coming week?"

"Oh, that's not necessary. I'd like a little more time to put the details together. . . ."

Just then an elderly lady sitting alone at a neighboring table broke in. "Are those French fried mushrooms good? They aren't greasy, are they, honey?"

Rhea picked up her plate of appetizers and held it out to the rather dowdy-looking woman. "Go ahead and try them," she said. "I think they're delicious."

Why was Rhea being so generous with their food? Hux wondered irritably as he watched the old lady wolf down most of the contents of the plate. He was hungry himself.

Rhea whispered, "I'm going to give her the rest too, Hux. She seems starved. Will you catch the waitress and order some more food for us—and her?"

"Okay." Now that he'd had a good look at her, Hux thought the lady appeared more eccentric than poor. Weren't those diamond rings on her greedy fingers? Starting to signal the waitress, he thought about Rhea's bountiful generosity. She was a real giver to friends—or strangers.

Then suddenly Hux had a brilliant idea. If a complete stranger could stir Rhea's sympathetic heart, then why couldn't he?

She liked to help people. She thrived on being warm and giving. That's why she'd been so kind to needy Jerry. Surely she'd help Hux too, if he needed it.

Perhaps *this* was the way to get to Rhea.

Hux could just imagine what it would be like to win Rhea's affections. He could picture her listening to him sympathetically, holding his hand and gazing sweetly into his eyes. And while she was doing that, he'd move his other hand around her shoulders and lower his mouth onto her luscious lips. Tender kisses would lead to more torrid ones, caresses would grow bolder . . . and then in some secluded nook with only soft music and the sound of their heartbeats to accompany their passionate lovemaking, he'd have Rhea completely in his power!

He could win her! He was sure of it.

"Why are you sitting there with your arm half-raised and that faraway look in your eyes?" Rhea asked with amusement. "You'll never get the waitress's attention that way."

Starting guiltily, Hux waved the waitress over.

As Rhea ordered, Hux wondered what would be the best approach for getting her to feel sorry for him. He certainly couldn't claim financial problems or unemployment—or ask her over to alter a suit for him. But there had to be *something* he could tell her to win her sympathy.

"Are you all right?" Rhea asked. "Your attention really seems to have wandered."

"Oh, I'm fine. I was just thinking of that old woman," he said, a plan forming in his mind. He sighed deeply. "Seeing someone so alone—so lonely —made me think how terrible life can be sometimes."

Rhea nodded somberly. "I think we should always

48

be sensitive to the plight of those who are less well off."

"I agree. But poverty can be emotional as well as physical," Hux told her, his scheme falling right into place. "Sometimes people are deprived and we don't even know it. They can be starving for affection, understanding, and real caring."

"The kind they should get from friends and family," Rhea murmured.

"Yes. And sometimes even those people let them down." Intentionally lowering his eyes to stare at his hands, folded on the table, he said, "It's so hard to talk about it."

"About what?" Rhea asked kindly, putting her hand over his encouragingly.

"Oh . . . about the way my family treated me." He sighed. "I've never really told anyone about it before. You know they kicked me out when I was thirteen? It was during a thunderstorm and I didn't even have a raincoat."

Rhea smiled. "Come on, Hux. That doesn't sound very likely. Is this a joke?"

"I'm telling the truth," he assured her.

She examined him closely, and her expression became serious. "That's just awful, Hux. You mean to say you've been living on your own since you were thirteen? How did you ever get an education? Prepare yourself for a job? Did you find work when your family kicked you out of the house?"

"Well, no. My family paid for me to go to boarding school."

"Boarding school?" Rhea asked, her voice sud-

49

denly suspicious. "And I suppose they made you walk there in the thunderstorm?"

"Well, not exactly," he stammered. "It was raining and the butler—who'd always *hated* me—savagely forced me into the limo and I was driven away. I'd already gotten wet because the wind was blowing and I hadn't been allowed to get a coat out of my suitcase. That was the worst September of my life."

"Now wait a minute!" Rhea insisted with a frown. "That doesn't sound deprived. I thought your family literally kicked you out."

"Well, it was the same thing, Rhea." Was his scheme backfiring? he wondered anxiously. "My parents never wanted me around because I got in the way of their traveling and parties. They weren't interested in a skinny kid like me or in family togetherness. I rarely even got to go home for holidays. When I complained about anything, my parents sent me off to another school. They liked to spend their time on more interesting, adult activities."

"But all of us have had problems with our families."

"Not problems like mine." A little desperate now, Hux said the first thing that sprang to mind. "How would you like it if your mother cursed the day you were born?"

"She what?"

Noting Rhea's skeptical look, Hux went on. "Well, she hasn't gone that far, literally, but that's the way she makes me feel—as if my birthday were an intrusion on her busy social schedule. She usually forgets the correct date and of course she has her personal secretary pick out and send my birthday gifts."

"She doesn't even call you?"

"Oh, she usually manages to get in touch a few days late. On my last birthday she was more interested in complaining about her own problems than hearing about me. It seems her secretary had just quit, so my gift had to wait until she took care of more important matters. After telling me that, she launched into a tirade on the difficulty of obtaining good help in this day and age. I never got a word in edgewise."

"That doesn't sound very caring, but you can't take it personally," Rhea said, patting Hux's hand comfortingly. "I'm sure your mother means well."

"I suppose so, but the scars last anyway," said Hux, starting to feel uneasy. He felt like he was on dangerous ground, but now that he had Rhea's attention he didn't want to lose it. "I rarely saw my parents or my younger sister after I was thirteen. I inherited money from my family, but I never got much love. I hate to admit it, Rhea, but I lead a lonely life."

She gazed at Hux's forlorn expression with new appreciation. He'd revealed the real sensitivity hidden under his cynical facade. She was quite touched that he had opened up to her this way.

But what could she say now to make him feel better? And why had he told *her* about his loneliness? Not knowing what to say, she reached across the table to grasp his hand. With a grateful smile he clasped her hand eagerly in return, intimately twining his fingers through hers. Chills ran up her arm as his thumb caressed her inner wrist and he transfixed her with vivid green eyes.

This wouldn't do at all! Rhea warned herself, will-

51

ing her heartbeat to slow down. In spite of her determination, his touch made electric thrills of excitement race through her. She knew she should pull away, but she couldn't bring herself to do so. Besides, a rejection might interrupt the flow of their important conversation. It was clear that Hux needed someone to talk to.

When the waitress brought the appetizers, Rhea reluctantly released Hux's hand so they could both eat. He moved closer to her and draped an arm over the back of her chair. She didn't object when he moved his hand lightly across her back, his long fingers stopping to rest beneath the fullness of her breast.

"All of us are lonely at times, Hux," she said rather breathlessly. "If you're not close to your family you can always turn to your friends."

"That's another problem. I have very few real friends. Why, just last year a couple of buddies of mine abandoned me in the wilderness."

"Really? Where?"

"Out in the wilds of Colorado—in the mountains. We'd gone on a skiing trip, and when I got hurt they went off and left me. It was terrible."

"They left you lying on the slopes?" Aware of his breath feathering her cheek and of his bold fingers caressing the underside of her breast, Rhea took a deep breath before asking "How were you rescued?"

"Huh?" Hux seemed to have lost track of his story. "Oh, the skiing accident. Well, luckily my ankle was only sprained, not broken. One of the resort's employees helped me limp back to the ski lodge."

"Resort? Where were you? I thought you said you were in the wilderness."

"Well, it's pretty wild in places around Aspen."

"Hux, a ski resort is not exactly the wilderness," said Rhea, stiffening. She noticed that his exploring fingers froze immediately. "I'm sorry, but I don't think that sounds so awful."

"It wasn't the resort that was bad. It was the fact that my friends went off and left me. I didn't see them the entire time we were there. They partied and skied and didn't care a thing about me. They're both prominent jet-setting lawyers," he said cynically. "I suppose they would have been more solicitous if I'd told them I wanted to sue my ski equipment manufacturer. As it was, I had to sit around by myself with my foot wrapped up, staring at the fire."

Noticing a flash of real anger in Hux's eyes, she said, "But there are other people around in a ski lodge. Couldn't you have made new acquaintances?"

"I tried to, believe me. There were a lot of people around who invited me to their rooms for get-togethers. But if I hadn't shown up, they'd never have noticed."

"There had to be some nice people somewhere in the crowd."

"Well, a few women brought me hot drinks and talked to me," he confessed.

"Women?" she asked. "How lonely could you be with them around?"

"Come on, Rhea. I really was alone," Hux said. "Those women weren't truly friendly or sympathetic. They liked my looks and wanted to make my acquaintance for a night or two, then leave without a

53

backward glance—unless they could make use of my connections. They were like a lot of other women I know."

Irritably remembering Hux's reputation, Rhea decided to give him some advice. "You may be attracting people like that, Hux. You need to be more particular about your choice of friends. You're going to have to change your behavior—delve beneath the surface and quit chasing pretty faces—if you really want some deeper attachment."

"What do you mean by that?" Hux demanded. "It sounds like you're blaming *me* for everything. Who says I went after so many women? Maybe they chased me until they got what they wanted, then left on their own account. I've suffered."

"I'm sure you have. But judging from what you've told me, you're never going to feel any better until you change yourself. Then people will treat you differently. You can't replace real attachment with trendy connections. That's an empty way to live. Change starts from within."

"My life-style isn't that empty!" Hux exclaimed testily, hurt and insulted by Rhea's advice. He'd never intended for this to happen, but almost in spite of himself he'd ended up revealing genuine feelings he'd never shared with anyone else. It was unsettling to know how close to the truth many of his "lies" had come. He didn't want to admit that often he really *was* lonely. He felt uncomfortable letting her believe him. He'd have to retrace his steps quickly in order to regain a modicum of pride.

Defensively, he said, "I utilize my social position to

54

do my job. The fact that I don't live exactly like you doesn't make me an empty human being."

"You were the one who indicated you were unhappy," Rhea pointed out.

"Okay, so I exaggerated," Hux admitted impatiently. "I'm happy with my life in spite of how it sounds. Maybe I embroidered a few details to make it sound worse than it really is."

Rhea was stunned. "Exaggerate? Embroider? You mean you've been lying?" Taking hold of the hand still resting against her side, Rhea pushed it away. "You're not unhappy? Not lonely?"

He gave her a lighthearted grin. "I did a good job of convincing you, huh?"

Rhea's amber eyes flared. "You've done a better job of making a fool of me. Why did you say those things, Hux?"

"Well . . . I wasn't trying to fool you exactly. I just wanted to form an attachment . . . get closer to you." Surely she'd be sympathetic to that, Hux thought.

"Closer in what way?" Rhea asked angrily. "I believed every word of your elaborate spiel. Did you think I'd be impressed to find out it's an act?" Glaring at him, she suddenly stood and grabbed her wrap. Then she started to walk away, muttering, "I should have known never to trust you!"

"Wait a minute!" Hux exclaimed, following her. "I was attracted to you and got carried away trying to make you feel something for me. What's so bad about that? And I really am lonely sometimes," he admitted.

"I don't want to hear anymore."

"You can't leave until we set a time to work on the video."

"I'll do it myself. It was my idea."

"No, it wasn't," Hux told her. "It was mine."

"Embroidering the truth again?" she countered angrily.

"Rhea, you know I suggested it first. You can't do the video without me."

"I can do anything I want! The Hidden Woman is my business."

"You mean you'd actually steal ideas?" he asked, angry himself. "Is that any more honest than my appealing to your sympathies with a few exaggerations?"

"The idea was mine!" Rhea cried, slamming the door in his face.

"No, it was mine!" Hux called as though she could still hear him.

Thoroughly aggrieved, he stood staring at the door. Damn! Wouldn't you know they'd end up in a fight just when he'd had Rhea almost completely in his power. If only the conversation hadn't started making him feel so awful, he would never have admitted how true his words were. He could've kept up the act and gotten his way.

Deciding he might as well go, Hux looked around for the waitress. Then, searching for loose change in his pockets, he decided to give one of his friends a call. After the frustrating time with Rhea—and the depressing details he'd given her—he could use some friendly diversion.

And he actually did have some real friends, didn't

he? Not everyone wanted to make use of his connections. He thought hard.

Let's see, there was Alan Kingsley—but he lived in California now and Hux hadn't seen him in a long time. And there was Michael Lewis and his wife—but Hux couldn't remember the last time he'd visited them. He sighed, feeling more lonely than ever.

Of course Rafe and Melissa liked him. Hux wondered if they'd mind if he came over to their place tonight. Rafe had been his best friend since college days, and although his wife Melissa always teased Hux about his glossy life-style, he knew she truly cared. Hux knew he could count on Rafe and Melissa to cheer him up.

Quickly finding the bar's pay phone, he dropped change into the slot, savoring thoughts of the evening ahead. He'd probably stay late at Rafe's. They would sit and talk after dinner, maybe even play a game of cards.

It'll be great, he thought, listening to the phone ring. The evening would fly by. But somehow the thought of returning to his empty apartment at all that night didn't appeal to Hux.

He wondered if Rafe and Melissa would let him sleep on their couch.

CHAPTER FOUR

"Excuse me," Hux drawled as Rhea almost ran into him coming out of June Sterling's door.

On her way into the vice-president's office, Rhea paused to give Hux a cold look. Then she quickly brushed past him to sit down, her heart pounding. It had barely been a week since their last encounter and she still felt shaky around him.

Glancing from Hux to Rhea, June spoke, "Since the two of you are together, I can tell you how much I liked the ideas for a fashion video you both submitted. Perhaps you can work together . . ."

Rhea interrupted June. "I doubt it. I'm sure Hux and I don't think alike at all."

Looking from Rhea to Hux, June seemed perplexed. Then she told them, "It wouldn't be my prerogative to choose between your ideas. That would be up to the executive board."

"Fine with me," Hux muttered.

"Mine was only a basic outline," said Rhea, shifting uncomfortably in her chair. She flashed Hux a look, but he just stood there staring at her, an odd expression on his handsome face. "Once I expand on it I'll submit it to the executive board, if that's what you want. I'm willing to accept their decision about whose idea they'll use."

Trying to beat Hux to the punch, Rhea had put together a sketchy outline for the project last week and had taken it to the vice-president first thing Monday morning. To her irritation, Rhea had learned that Hux had done the very same thing. Now that June had suggested they submit their competing ideas to the board, it made Rhea feel they were vying for a prize in some silly contest.

Propping his lean frame against the door, Hux told June, "I'm still working on my video idea too. I think it's good, but I'm willing to listen to what the board says."

"I'm sure they'll make a fair decision," said Rhea, hoping the store's executives would see that she was the one who best knew how to display fashion.

"May the best person win," said Hux, flashing the easy grin that had always irritated Rhea. Then, giving her one last glance, he turned on his heel and strode away.

"It's unfortunate you and Hux don't want to work together," said June, her sharp eyes sparkling. "Combining both your talents would make the project twice as good."

"We'll have lots of other projects to work on," said Rhea, knowing eventually she would have to get over the anxiety of dealing with Hux. If only she didn't feel so drawn to him, everything would be much easier. But when their eyes had met earlier, electric sparks had seemed to pass between them. Wasn't there some way to shut off the current? Rhea wondered. She knew the only way to accomplish that was to stay as far away from Hux as she could.

"The name is Huxley Benton," Hux said, looking up at the tall black man who'd opened the door of the Soho loft. "Ngamé sent me an invitation to her party. I'm a guest."

"Huxley?" growled the man in a deep voice. He didn't smile as he took a sheet of paper out of his jacket pocket. "There's no Huxley on this list. The only name beginning with *H* is Halsey Bacon. You can't crash this party, buster."

"Ngamé knows me, honest." The black man scowled at him so fiercely, Hux was sure he was going to have the door slammed in his face. Then Ngamé herself rushed from the kitchen with a heaping tray of food.

"George! Let him in," shouted the designer, hardly pausing for a second. "Hi, Halsey! Talk to you later."

"Okay, Mr. Bacon," George mumbled under his breath. "Some people get so drunk they don't even know their own names." Looking down at Hux with a sardonic eye, he ordered, "Give me your coat. I'm going to put it up on the bedroom level, but don't you go up there. If you want to leave, let me know."

"Sure," Hux agreed, not wishing to bicker over a small thing like his name. Was George Ngamé's bodyguard? Trying to be friendly, he asked, "Didn't you used to play professional basketball or football or something?"

"Yeah," the man said before lumbering away.

As George departed, Hux turned his thoughts to Rhea Mitchell. Knowing Ngamé was her good friend, he was certain he'd run into Rhea tonight. Looking forward to that, Hux straightened the sleeves of his elegant evening jacket over his immaculate shirt cuffs and eagerly set off across the long expanse of polished wooden floor.

As he followed the sound of music and laughter and talk, Hux quickly surveyed his surroundings. The loft was divided by gently curving partitions that defined alcoves. Raised levels served as cozy living areas. Most of the walls were painted a neutral sand color, while a few glowed with the wilder hues of purple, magenta, and red. Exotic tapestries and prints from around the world hung everywhere. A large number of potted plants—leafy palms and tall ficus trees—grew in a veritable forest near the center of the loft. On the other side of this jungle Hux found the other guests.

Searching the faces of those eagerly helping themselves to a generous buffet, he was surprised to recognize only a couple of people from the media. The others were not from his usual crowd. And where was Rhea?

"Halsey!" Ngamé said, coming up behind him. Hux swung around to see the black woman glide across the floor in a silken caftan of vivid indigo blue. Her golden earrings, bracelets, and necklaces sparkled in the glow of the loft's suffused lighting.

"Uh, it's Huxley . . . Hux," he told her.

"Oh, okay. Whatever. I'm glad you could come. George said I should invite someone special for Rhea. She'll be happy to see you."

"She will?"

"Sure. I told her I was inviting you. She's in the kitchen at the moment."

"Well, great. I'll go talk to her," said Hux, feeling pleased. Obviously wanting to make up, Rhea must have hinted who the "someone special" should be. She must have gotten over her anger at his exaggerations. Rhea hadn't seemed friendly when they'd met a few days ago in June's office, but maybe she preferred to see him alone.

"There's Rhea—she's bringing out some wine," Ngamé said. "Rhea, here's Hartley!"

Expecting to see an expression of welcome on Rhea's lovely face, Hux instead watched her eyes grow huge and her mouth drop open in what looked like severe shock. Losing her grip on an armful of bottles, Rhea almost dropped them on the floor.

"Watch it, girl. Champagne's not supposed to be shaken up like that."

Ngamé headed over to help her friend. Instead of taking the bottles to the buffet, however, Rhea muttered something and both women disappeared behind a cluster of plants.

On their way back to the kitchen, Rhea hissed, "What the . . . What's *he* doing here?"

"Hartley? I told you I was inviting him."

"You said nothing of the sort. You didn't mention Huxley Benton to me," Rhea said accusingly.

Ngamé looked confused. "Huxley?" She shrugged. "I thought you'd be happy if I provided you with a handsome escort for the evening."

"Escort? Hux and I don't even get along. How could you do this to me?" Rhea complained. Glaring

62

at her friend as they entered the kitchen, she placed the champagne on a counter.

"Settle down. I've never known you to get in such a state. What's so bad about the guy?" asked Ngamé. "He seemed real happy to see you."

"He was probably thinking about another trick he could play on me."

"Tricks?" A sly smile curved Ngamé's lips. "Say, are you in love? Did you two have a spat?"

"Certainly not! How could I be in love? You don't know what that man's done to get to me," Rhea explained, trying to make Ngamé understand. She wished she'd told her about the problems she'd been having with Hux all along. "He's a . . . monstrous liar. He's always scheming and trying to con me. I never know what he's going to do next."

"Sounds interesting. Maybe it's love and you don't even know it." Ngamé handed Rhea a wineglass. "Why don't you have a drink and go talk to him?"

"Good God, no!" Rhea cried, at her wits' end.

Just then Hux sauntered into the kitchen's doorway, a sexy grin on his face. "Don't worry," he told Rhea. "Whatever's wrong, old Hux is here to help. I won't let Ngamé load you up with all those heavy bottles again. I'll carry them out myself."

"I'm so grateful," Rhea said sarcastically.

But Hux chose to ignore her snide tone.

Ngamé paid no attention to Rhea's imploring look. Beaming benevolently at Hux, the black woman handed him the champagne along with a large bucket of ice. "I think I'll go find George and leave you two alone," she said. "Enjoy!"

Rhea took a long, deep breath. What was she going to do?

Arms loaded, obviously intending to return to the party area, Hux looked at her questioningly. Deciding to face the inevitable graciously, Rhea grabbed some more wineglasses and accompanied him.

"That's a gorgeous dress you have on," he told her, running his gaze appreciatively along the curves accentuated by a floor-length panne velvet gown with a low, drapey neckline and dolman sleeves.

"Thanks. It's new."

"That green-on-green print looks positively snaky. Are you trying to tempt me in this garden of Eden?" Hux asked as they edged past the jungle of plants.

"Sure. But you'd better watch out for my fangs. I might be tempted to bite."

"Wow, sounds kinky. Are you going to let me have a bite too—of your apple?"

"That's forbidden fruit. Remember what happened to Adam."

"Oh, Lord, no!" Hux stared up at the ceiling in mock alarm, as if he expected a lightning bolt to descend at any moment.

Rhea had to smile. If nothing else, the man was amusing. Even so, she didn't want to be "escorted" by him all evening. She preferred to socialize with the rest of the guests so she scanned the gathering, her full lips curving as she saw someone she knew. Waving enthusiastically, she gushed, "Hi, Marge!"

"Rhea!" cried Marge, a small vivacious brunette. She hurried over. "I haven't seen you in such a long time. What have you been doing?"

Depositing the champagne bottles on the end of

the buffet table, Hux watched Rhea greet her friend. Face animated, graceful hands gesturing, she acted as if Marge was intensely important to her. Hux moved next to Rhea, patiently waiting to be introduced. But she didn't even look at him.

"I'm opening my consulting service at Haldan-Northrop," Rhea told her friend.

"How exciting!" said Marge, giving Hux a curious look. "I've always thought I ought to consult you. Can you advise short people too?"

"I certainly can."

"Maybe I should make an appointment sometime."

"Whenever it would be convenient for you."

Insulted by Rhea's ignoring him, Hux decided to take matters into his own hands. "Marge," he blurted, aiming his most disarming smile at her. "Rhea's told me all about you and I have to admit you're just as attractive as she's said. I'm Huxley Benton."

With gratification Hux watched the small woman blush. She stammered, "Oh, really? How do you do?"

"I work with Rhea at Haldan-Northrop," he went on. "I don't want to discourage her business, but why do you think you need a consultation? You obviously already know how to dress."

As Marge turned a deeper shade of crimson, Hux glanced at Rhea out of the corner of his eye. She was flushed too, but it wasn't with embarrassment. Her amber eyes glowed, banked with golden fire.

"Hux and I met at Haldan-Northrop, Marge," said Rhea sweetly. "He runs the store's charm school. He just gave you a sample of what you can learn there—

how to offer superficial compliments at a moment's notice."

Hux hastened to reassure the woman. "I meant everything I said, Marge. And I'm sorry I interrupted. It's just that Rhea's upset because we've had a disagreement."

"I think I'd better leave you two," mumbled Marge.

"No," objected Rhea. She opened her mouth to say something else, but her friend was already hurrying off.

"Oh, no!" she told Hux. "Now her feelings are hurt. Look what you've done!"

"I've done nothing but make sure we're alone."

"Well, we won't be for long. I came here to socialize, not argue with you."

"Who wants to argue?" Hux asked meaningfully.

But Rhea had turned her back and was weaving her way through the increasingly crowded area. While they'd been talking, dozens of new guests had arrived. The music was louder now and some couples were dancing.

Weaving his way after Rhea, Hux wondered why she insisted on playing hard to get. Ngamé had as much as said Rhea found him special, so why was she running away?

When he caught up with her again, Rhea was helping herself to the buffet and talking to Vivian Collins, one of the guests Hux knew, a food critic from *Bon Palate* magazine.

"Isn't this a wonderful spread?" Vivian asked Rhea, gesturing at the feast. "It's exciting to count more exotic foods than one can identify. Do you know what this dish is?"

"It's some kind of Moroccan dip—made of chick peas, I think."

"Oh, a form of hummus? It's certainly an unusual color." Vivian dipped a small piece of pita bread into the mixture and tasted it.

Taking a plate and squeezing into line beside Rhea, Hux said to the two women, "That stuff is good, isn't it? I predict North African food will be as big a trend as sushi."

"I'll believe it if you say so, Hux," said Vivian, glancing at him. "You ought to know."

"Shall I write down his prediction so we can check on it in a few months?" Rhea asked the woman. "Or is he forecasting for the next year?"

"Why don't you ask him? Hux is knowledgeable about everything new," said Vivian.

Disgruntled, Rhea moved along slowly, adding items to her plate at random. It looked as if she wasn't going to keep Hux from joining her. He was almost breathing down her neck. But that didn't mean she wouldn't fight him.

"Personally, I prefer to start trends, not predict them," said Rhea crossly, stabbing at some spicy marinated mushrooms. "I like to combine various elements and create my own special mix." Trying to ignore the sensations Hux caused when his thigh rubbed against her own, she helped herself to salmon mousse, curried chicken, and some kiwi.

"Are those the ingredients for the Rhea Mitchell special?" Hux asked, his warm breath feathering her cheek.

67

"Could be." In reaction to his challenge, and trying to get her mind off his nearness, Rhea placed a small amount of each ingredient on a large wheat cracker. She took a bite and chewed, and decided the flavor, if weird, wasn't all that bad.

"If you're trying to be creative," said Hux, "you've got a long way to go. Why not try something really adventurous?"

Placing his plate on the table, he heaped various ingredients on a piece of flat Syrian bread—raw ginger, bean curd, slices of fried sweet potato, and what looked like sardines. Tearing off a corner, he tasted the concoction while people on either side of him watched curiously.

Leaning forward to spoon on additional ingredients, Rhea said, "I think it would be even better if you added a few more things. Why not try some of the pickled octopus, chili peppers, anchovies, and a few kumquats?"

"Wait a minute. That piece of bread won't hold much more."

"Don't you mean to say you're afraid to eat what's on it?" She almost laughed at his dismayed expression.

"I'd like to see you try it."

"I'll taste it, if you will."

"You're on, Rhea. Who's going to take the first bite?"

"We'll eat at the same time."

Cutting the bread raggedly and folding up the ends, Rhea lifted her half of the curious sandwich to her lips. When she saw Hux taste his half, she took a huge bite. Odd textures and flavors exploded against her tongue—sweet, sour, salty, spicy, mingled with tastes she couldn't define—and didn't want to.

Quickly, Rhea swallowed.

"Aren't you going to eat the rest of it?" asked Hux, chewing casually.

"Of course."

But in a few minutes Rhea had had all she wanted of the buffet and scrambled away to get a glass of strong red wine to combat the lingering combination of flavors in her mouth. While taking long gulps, she noticed Hux wasn't beside her any longer.

Now was the right time to make another attempt at escaping his unwanted companionship. Rhea looked around. Hadn't she seen an old beau of hers wandering by a while ago? Holding on to another man would be the perfect defense against Hux.

Hurriedly, she scanned the people around her and then made her way toward a grouping of couches and chairs. With relief she sighted the large man sitting off by himself.

"Wallace," Rhea called. "How are you?"

"Rhea?" He lifted his shaggy brows. As she neared him, he rose to an impressive height and took her hands in his. "It's been a long time."

It must have been intuition that made Rhea abruptly glance behind her—to see Hux bearing down upon them. Thinking swiftly, she urged, "Why don't we dance, Wallace? For old times' sake."

"We never danced together. Don't you remember my two left feet?"

"Please? It'll be fun."

"Oh, all right," Wallace grumbled, giving her an appraising look.

The space that had been set aside for the dance floor was crowded, but Rhea managed to drag Wallace into the crush of moving bodies.

"It's been ages since I've seen you, Rhea. And I've missed you. Do you ever have any thoughts about getting back together?" Wallace asked, sounding hopeful as he moved clumsily against her.

Realizing she had put herself in an awkward situation, Rhea said, "I've always considered myself your friend."

"But you don't want any more than that?"

Rhea gazed up at him. "You know we already decided it would never work out, Wallace. Nothing has changed. But I still care for you."

He sighed, making Rhea feel guilty. She'd approached Wallace for selfish reasons and had probably disappointed the poor guy all over again. But who would have thought he'd still be interested after two years? About to suggest they leave the dance floor as the music changed from soft rock to a faster, wilder beat, she noticed Hux swing by with an attractive blonde.

"Hey, Rhea, who's your partner? Going to give Candy and me some competition?"

Ignoring him, Wallace complained to Rhea, "This music's too fast. I can't dance to it."

Moving expertly to the music, Hux said, "Just watch me, buddy. It's not so difficult."

"Don't pay any attention to him, Wallace," Rhea said, annoyed at the expertise of Hux and his pretty companion. "We can dance however we want. Try this." She showed her partner a few less strenuous moves, but when she let go of his hand to do a turn, Wallace stumbled and started to walk away.

"Please don't leave me alone out here," Rhea pleaded, pushing back the hair that had fallen in her face. "I'm having such a good time."

"Well . . . okay," Wallace mumbled.

Rhea glanced around to see the dance floor. She caught sight of Hux and his partner. To her irritation, she saw the infuriating fast-talker execute a professional-looking series of freestyle steps.

"Show off," she murmured under her breath. She held on to Wallace tightly, trying to avoid the triumphant grin on Hux's face.

"I've had enough of this," muttered Wallace with a sigh a few minutes later. "I'm sorry, Rhea, but you'll have to count me out."

Finding herself suddenly alone, Rhea scowled at Hux and started to walk away stiffly.

"Wait a minute," said Hux, approaching her. "Can't you find another partner?"

"No."

"Well, how about you and me teaming up then? Candy can rejoin her boyfriend."

"Yeah, that would be fun," agreed Candy.

"Come on, Rhea. We'll make good partners," said Hux. "I'd like to see you enjoy part of the evening."

"That's nice, considering you ruined the rest of it," Rhea snapped.

"Well, we would have had a lot more fun if you'd have avoided playing all these games you seem addicted to."

"*Me? I* play games?" Rhea could hardly believe her ears.

71

"Yes, you. You accused me of being the gamesman, but ever since we met, you've been hell-bent on playing at something or the other. I'd rather dance with you than Candy. If we're finished with all the competitive, amusing banter now, why don't we try another form of communication?"

Before Rhea could find her voice to reply, Hux took her hand and led her back to the dance floor. "Can you put on some salsa?" he called out to the disc jockey in charge of the music.

As the music began, Hux enfolded Rhea loosely in his arms and adroitly whirled her to the hypnotic rhythm of Latin music.

Feeling slightly dizzy—had she drunk too much wine?—Rhea let herself relax and follow his lead. Although she wouldn't admit it, she'd been wanting to do this ever since she'd seen how accomplished a dancer Hux was. And a little harmless diversion couldn't hurt their already problematic relationship.

Gazing at her approvingly, Hux clasped her more tightly. "You're a wonderful dancer," he whispered. Lifting her face to him, Rhea inhaled the unique fragrance of his cologne. His firm jaw was only inches from her nose, his lips so near she could imagine how they would feel covering her own. . . .

Without thinking, she ran her free hand over the velvety surface of his jacket collar. Hux responded by lightly stroking the small of her back, his exploring fingers leaving burning impressions that seemed to penetrate the soft fabric to the flesh beneath. Rhea couldn't help but lean toward him, eyes mesmerized by his hypnotic gaze. When his lips parted enticingly, she caught her breath.

72

Instead of kissing her, however, Hux drew back a little and spoke. "You're an incredibly sensuous woman, Rhea. But I want you to know I'm attracted to more than your luscious body and beautiful face. I'm crazy about *you*—I appreciate all the competitive, witty, warmhearted twists and turns of your intelligent mind." He regarded her earnestly. "I know I've done the wrong thing at times, but I haven't known how to approach you. Please believe I'm not feeding you a line now. I'm telling the truth."

Seeing him look so intense and sincere, Rhea blinked and tried to relieve the tension by joking. "You may be truthful, Hux, but you're not accurate. How can my mind be warmhearted? My heart's not located in my head."

Hux looked at her chest admiringly. "No, it's certainly not."

"You're impossible."

"So are you. That's another reason I like you." With that remark he swung her back into a dance step.

And Rhea went with him willingly, tuning in to the salsa's brassy, sexy rhythm and her partner's movements. The wordless rapport between them was overwhelmingly sensual. Wasn't that what had been getting to her since they'd first begun to dance? Hux was right about there being other forms of communication.

"Nice choice of music," called Ngamé, dancing by with her arms entwined about George's neck, the huge man moving lightly on his feet.

Rhea hardly heard her friend. She was lost in the spell of the moment. Rhea was aware only of the handsome man in her arms.

73

Embracing him fully, she detected the play of strong muscles beneath the silken fabric of his shirt. Her full breasts pressed against his chest as he pulled her to him securely, the movement making her nipples tighten and tingle with arousal. Thigh to thigh, his firm abdomen nestled against her softer one, she felt his own heightening romantic interest.

"Rhea," he breathed before his mouth descended and captured her own. Arching back wantonly, she let his tongue pry her lips apart and penetrate the recesses within. Skillfully, she used her own tongue to tease the invader with advances and retreats while one of Hux's eager hands moved lower on her hip.

"That salsa was sexy, wasn't it, George?" said Ngamé loudly from nearby. "Rhea and Hartley sure enjoyed it."

The voice was intrusive, as was the sudden lack of music. Slowly becoming aware of herself and the situation, Rhea placed her hands against Hux's chest and pushed gently against him. Held at arm's length, he looked startled, his green eyes slightly foggy.

"The music has stopped," Rhea told him, her face flushing with embarrassment. "And I think I'd better go home."

"I'll be more than happy to go with you," Hux replied.

CHAPTER FIVE

Rhea stepped off an icy curb and climbed nervously into the backseat of a dilapidated taxi. She felt her heartbeat accelerate as Hux slid in beside her and rattled off her Manhattan address. She wrapped her foxtail-trimmed velvet cape around her securely as though it would soothe the anxieties that had developed as the cold night air cleared her overheated brain.

Was she being foolish in allowing the promotions director to accompany her home? Now admitting her tremendous attraction to the man, Rhea was happily aware the feeling was mutual. No doubt Huxley Benton would make another pass before she alighted from the vehicle, and the thought excited her.

Ngamé had been urging her to find a new man. Could it be that Hux was the one?

"Ngamé really knows how to give a party," Hux said as he slipped an arm across the back of the seat, distracting Rhea by lightly touching her shoulder with the tips of his fingers. "I like her. She's really dynamic. She and that George guy make a striking couple on the dance floor. They should get together, you know?"

"They already have," Rhea answered after taking a deep breath to steady her voice. "They've been going together for more than three years."

"Really? A long-term relationship. That's nice," he said thoughtfully.

"Many people believe in that sort of thing."

"And many people don't," Hux said quietly. "Well, now I know why Ngamé and George dance so well together. They've had a lot of practice." He slipped his arm around Rhea . . . his lips brushing the loose curls that fell over her forehead. "That was the best party I've been to in years."

"You do like to dance, don't you?" Rhea whispered unevenly, slightly dizzy from his wonderful masculine scent.

"I do love to dance, especially when I have a worthy partner. But that's not what I'm talking about. The people seemed so . . . real."

Rhea chuckled. "I hope so. I don't think they've perfected androids yet."

"I don't know. If you went to some of the parties I do, you might think they had."

Rhea almost asked him why he attended social gatherings frequented by shallow people, but the unpleasant thought reminded her of Hux's "loneliness" scam. Not wanting to be angry again, especially since he'd apologized, she pushed the memory away and concentrated instead on his hand which was lightly stroking her leg just above the knee.

The taxi swerved around a corner and Rhea slid hard into Hux. His hand accidentally slipped a little higher into the slit of her dress, but she didn't push it

76

away. Feeling her firm flesh tremble under his finger-tips, Hux smiled.

She made him believe in things he'd begun to think he'd never find. Warmth. Caring. Selflessness. Was it some kind of miracle that allowed a nurturing, down-to-earth woman like Rhea Mitchell to be attracted to a slick guy like Huxley Benton?

Hux no longer wanted to concoct new schemes to trick the warmhearted woman into seeing him. She'd become more than a prize in a cat-and-mouse game. Though he couldn't exactly define how, Rhea had become vitally important to his well-being, and Hux was afraid that if he did or said the wrong thing one more time, he'd forever lose the chance to be with her.

For one crazy moment Hux thought of telling Rhea his feelings, but that would mean explaining that his revelations about his lonely life had been true. He could never do that, Hux thought, not without severely damaging his pride.

Barely able to breathe for all the spectacular sensations running through her, Rhea was thankful when the taxi pulled over to the curb in front of her apartment building and Hux had to move his hand to pay the driver. She couldn't think straight when he was touching her, and Rhea knew she had a lot of thinking to do—about him.

Yet when Hux got out of the taxi and said, "I'll see you safely up to your apartment," she didn't even murmur the smallest objection.

They passed the doorman and entered the elevator. "What floor?"

"Nineteen."

"Hmm. My lucky number."

Hux surrounded her, his hands propped against the elevator wall on either side of her head. She stared into his amused green eyes and watched them come closer before allowing her lids to drift shut.

Her lips parted, receiving his eagerly. Hux's kiss was soft, sweet, and so seductive!

How had she resisted this for so long?

Resistance was the last thing on Rhea's mind as she kissed Hux in return, stroking his tongue with her own. Thrills of anticipation ran through her body, alerting her to the fact that kisses wouldn't quench the rapidly growing desire spreading through her like wildfire. The delicious sensation was heightened by their rapid ascent toward her apartment.

But when the elevator stopped, Rhea was too engrossed in the heady taste and feel of Hux to break the embrace. The doors swished open, then closed once more, and the elevator went on. The tingling intensified, and when Rhea felt Hux's hands exploring beneath her cape, she thought she might explode.

The elevator paused, then descended, the change in motion urging Rhea into Hux, pressing her breasts against his knowing hands. Her nipples tightened beneath the velvet dress, and Hux groaned. He nudged her thighs apart and leaned into her, slipping a leg through the slit of her skirt. Splaying his hands over her full bottom, Hux pulled her into him, hard. Rhea recognized the proof of his arousal against her belly, felt her own body respond to it, and knew she was ready for him.

Suddenly the elevator stopped, and this time when

the doors opened, a middle-aged man strolled in and asked, "Going down?"

Though Hux pulled away casually, as though they had been doing nothing out of the ordinary, Rhea blushed. "Uh, yes. Nineteen, please," she told him, keeping her eyes straight ahead on the closing doors.

"You already passed it," the stranger told her, amusement in his voice. He pushed the lobby button and the elevator sped downward. "That was fourteen."

"Oh."

Hux slipped a comforting arm around Rhea's waist, but she was still embarrassed. The man was watching them as though he expected a good show. Good Lord, what had come over her? Why had she allowed things to get out of hand so quickly?

" 'Bye now," the stranger said with a grin as he left the elevator.

Hux pressed nineteen once more before turning to Rhea with a mischievous twinkle in his eyes. "Now, where were we?"

Rhea frowned at Hux as he moved in on her. "You were supposed to be seeing me to my door."

"Didn't you like the way I was doing it?"

Blushing again, Rhea moved away and muttered, "I didn't say I didn't, but I'd like to get to my apartment some time tonight."

"Your apartment would be more comfortable," Hux told her agreeably.

That statement made Rhea's pulse skip a beat. Hux didn't sound like he was planning to leave! Things were going a little too fast for her. Though Rhea enjoyed earthy pleasures as well as any red-blooded woman, she'd never been aroused so thoroughly so quickly, and she wasn't sure what to do about it.

"After you," Hux said as the doors opened on her floor.

Rhea preceded him, nervously extracting her keys from her evening bag. Would Hux launch another sensual assault on her? Would she have the will to resist if he did?

"Let me." His husky voice made Rhea shiver as he took the keys from her nerveless fingers. "I'm glad I listened to my protective instincts and brought you home."

"So am I."

"Well, we agree on something."

Hux was standing there in front of the open door, making no move to enter. Rhea took a deep breath. "We could agree on more things if you'd make an effort," she said reasonably.

"That goes both ways."

"What's that supposed to mean?"

"That you enjoy arguing."

"Well, I like a lively conversation."

"It's called arguing."

Aggravation dispelling her passionate mood, Rhea exclaimed, "Look who's talking!"

"At the moment we both are."

"But I'm not the one who uses tricks to get what I want."

"Oh, stop arguing, would you?" Hux muttered, doing the only thing he figured would make her.

Yet the moment his lips touched Rhea's, Hux called himself every kind of fool. He should have left while the going was good. He was pretty sure Rhea wasn't ready for more intimacy than they'd shared in the elevator, but what she was doing to his body was downright sinful! Hux broke off the embrace abruptly.

She blinked twice. Then her lids lowered and her expression changed. She seemed to struggle with some decision. When he stepped back, Rhea softly murmured, "Wouldn't you like to come inside . . . for a drink?"

"I'm not thirsty."

She glanced up at him. "Something to eat?"

"Not hungry."

Now she was boldly looking him in the eye, her expression bemused, her voice low and deliberately sexy. "An apple?"

Hux chuckled. "I could be tempted. Now who's using tricks?"

"Tricks?" she asked, suddenly all innocence. "I'm merely trying to show my appreciation for your protective instincts."

Following Rhea into her apartment, Hux felt as nervous as a kid. Irrationally, he felt as if his life's happiness rested on the outcome of this night, and he sure as hell didn't want to screw things up. The possibility made his mouth go dry.

"Actually, I am thirsty, Rhea. A glass of wine would be nice."

He didn't like her wicked little smile when she said, "I'll be right back."

She disappeared through a swinging door, and Hux looked around the living area. It was much like the woman—lush and exotic, yet warm and comfortable.

81

The unusual colors, antiques, and modern furniture blended into a pleasing whole.

A heavy wooden desk in the dining alcove contrasted with the softly illuminated open shelving that separated the work area from the rest of the living space. Glass shelves held objets d'art—baskets, pottery, small figures, some of which looked like museum pieces. A chocolate-covered modern couch was set off by peach, gold, turquoise, and deep green pillows. Under it, a peach Chinese rug with pale turquoise flowers covered a portion of the parquet flooring. A wonderful array of flowering plants thrived along the floor-to-ceiling-windowed wall.

The room's atmosphere and coloring matched the three Rousseau prints framed and hung on the deep green walls.

One of the Rousseaus inspired an erotic vision of Rhea lying on her bed nude, her arms spread wide in welcome. To get his mind off the luscious image, Hux quickly turned his attention to the next print—of a voluptuous, hypnotic-eyed woman with a flute. There was a snake wrapped around her, while another peered out from leafy, deep-green foliage.

"Do you like *The Snake Charmer?*" Rhea asked, returning from the kitchen.

"I've always liked primitive art."

"Undoubtedly because it's so sensual."

"You must have a thing about snakes. I noticed that bronze on your shelf," Hux said, referring to a statue of a woman with a snake in each hand.

"That's a replica of the snake goddess from ancient Crete."

Then Hux noticed she was carrying a tray with a

bottle of wine and glasses, a couple of peaches, a bunch of grapes . . . and an apple sliced into eight perfect wedges.

Pretending not to notice, he said, "These paintings remind me of the Garden of Eden. Very appealing."

"You'll find the nearest Eden out the windows." Rhea set the tray on a carved-wood coffee table inlaid with shells. "Central Park."

"It's a jungle out there all right, with all kinds of strange creatures sneaking around at this time of night."

"I try not to let the local wildlife bother me," Rhea told him as she sat and poured the wine.

"I guess we're safe enough in your exotic tower."

"And the view from here is spectacular, especially in spring or summer."

"I hope I get the chance to see it sometime," Hux said while thinking the view inside was spectacular enough.

He was unable to tear his gaze away from the slit in her dress, where Rhea's long legs were revealed to mid-thigh. Imagining the ecstasy of having those luscious legs wrapped around his back, Hux felt himself flush.

"Whew! It's warm in here," he said immediately, to cover the color he knew was rising on his neck.

"You could take off your jacket."

Relieved, Hux stripped off his jacket, then took his wine and strolled over to the window.

What was he thinking? Rhea wondered, longingly inspecting him. He was such a beautiful man—blond, tanned, good profile, perfect body. Not that there was anything wrong with the way she looked, Rhea immediately assured herself. But then, if Hux was attracted to her, why was he standing over there by the window?

She'd decided impulsively to tease him with the apple, not planning how the evening would end. Then it would be his move, but Rhea didn't think Hux would make one. Well, she certainly wasn't going to, Rhea decided even as she heard herself ask, "Wouldn't you like something to go with that wine?"

"What did you have in mind?"

Grinning, Rhea held out a wedge of the fruit in question. Hux came toward her, lowered his head, and took the apple with his teeth. Her grin dissolved as his lips brushed her fingers and her hand caught fire. Their eyes met, and she was snared anew by the sexual tension between them.

Rhea wasn't sure who made the first move, but suddenly they were in each other's arms, kissing deeply. His tongue played with hers, then he brushed her throat with his mouth. He burrowed his face in her cleavage and his hot moist kisses made the tops of her breasts sizzle.

In return, she ran her fingers over his back and down his neck while pressing herself closer. Pushing up on one full breast so that it threatened to spill from her dress, Hux nuzzled away the velvet material and the skimpy lace underneath. His tongue found the nipple already hardened into an aching peak. Rhea trembled and sighed deeply.

"Rhea Mitchell, you are the sexiest woman I've ever met," he told her in a strained voice. "If I don't leave now, I won't be able to."

"Oh" was all she said, but Hux thought he heard a

small echo of disappointment in the single throaty syllable.

Did she want him to stay? Unwilling to leave before he found out, he said lightly, "I wonder which of us is the snake and which the charmer. I wouldn't mind playing the snake if I could wrap myself around your luscious body."

Hesitating only a few seconds, Rhea rose slowly and held out her hand.

Taking it, Hux allowed her to lead him through the bedroom doorway. Rhea adjusted a dimmer, and the room was softly illuminated by torchlike wall lamps. His gaze was drawn immediately to the platform bed with its enveloping fall of draped material, splashes of deep turquoise and rich copper orange against peach walls.

He was drawn to the bed like a magnet, and now it was he who led Rhea. Then he turned his attention to the wide-eyed woman beside him. Her breathing was ragged and there was a doubtful expression on her lovely face, as though she were having second thoughts. Hux placed a soft kiss on her trembling lower lip.

"Undress me, Rhea."

Obeying his whispered command as though she could not deny him, Rhea unbuttoned his shirt, yet avoided his eyes as if she'd suddenly grown shy. Though he could tell she was being careful not to touch him any more than she had to, Hux thought her undressing of him was the most sensuous experience of his life. He could see Rhea was equally affected. Her hands definitely trembled as she tugged at his briefs and found him fully aroused. Then Hux helped her, impatient to be rid of his clothing so he could remove hers.

He quickly found the catch that allowed the velvet dress to unwrap, but he didn't strip it from her. Instead, he slipped Rhea's hose and lace briefs past her hips, then pushed her down to the bed and knelt to remove the undergarments.

Feeling she was still in doubt, Hux decided to loosen her up with a touch of whimsy. "I love the colors of this room. They spark my imagination. I can almost see you floating in a lagoon of deep turquoise with a copper-orange sun beating down."

He felt her relax before answering. "Hmm. Our very own paradise."

She smiled so sexily that it made Hux's heart skip a beat. Trailing his fingers up her firm calves, along her fleshy inner thighs, and around her voluptuous hips, he likened Rhea's form to those of the ancient statues he'd seen in Greece. But unlike those women of stone she was soft and warm and welcoming. When he undid the front clasp of her lace bra, her full breasts spilled out into his hands, and he felt her life-force for himself.

"I've never wanted anything so much in my life. You're so beautiful—an ancient goddess luring me to do her bidding in a jungle paradise," Hux murmured before lowering his head to taste her.

Rhea closed her eyes, content now that she hadn't made a mistake in leading Hux here. He made her feel special to him, and from the way he touched her, she knew he'd be a considerate lover.

How long could she take the delicious torture to her sensitive nipples? Yet Hux had barely begun.

When he pushed her back against the bed, she parted her legs, expecting him to join her. Instead, he tantalized her with slow, hot kisses, trailing them down her stomach to the insides of her thighs. Tangling her fingers in his hair, she tried to pull him up.

"I thought you were going to wrap yourself around me," she whispered urgently.

"All in good time" was all he said, otherwise ignoring her plea.

Nipping the inside of her thighs until she arched to him, Hux moaned—a very satisfied sound, Rhea thought—then found the heart of her passion. The stroke of his tongue made her realize how close she was to release. She tugged on his hair again, but still he ignored her. Then she was lost in sensation, unable to fight and take her lover with her, losing herself in the jungle fantasy he'd conjured with his teasing words.

The cool waters of the turquoise lagoon heated around her. The flaming ball of copper orange came closer and closer until it scorched her body. Rhea arched, accepting it gladly, losing herself in its burning heat. Stiffening, she cried out, calling Hux's name.

Suddenly he was next to her—pulling off her dress completely, tugging her farther up on the bed, kissing her, joining her. She thrust herself at him.

"Wait," he whispered. "If you move, I can't . . ."

But Rhea was too impatient. She wrapped her long legs around Hux's back and pressed herself to him, then heard him groan. Running her nails along his spine, she moved under him sensuously. Suddenly he hastened the pace, driving into her hard, and Rhea met his wild challenge until they were both panting and slick with sweat.

Hux's mouth closed over hers in an abandoned kiss unlike any she'd experienced, and though she knew her lips would be bruised and sore, she savored the embrace. When his fingers closed over one of her ultrasensitive nipples and tormented it, she cried out and arched into him harder. Then Hux tensed and loosened his mouth to whisper her name.

Rhea knew she was lost. Deep primitive colors whirled behind her eyelids, their frenzied movement ending in a brilliant explosion of blues and greens and magentas. She bit into the salty flesh of his shoulder and felt Hux shudder. He fell against her, crushing her into the mattress, but she received his weight gladly, tightening her legs around him. Then, still tangled, Hux rolled so they were both on their sides.

Rhea tenderly touched her lover's face, content to lie comfortably twined with him. Hux found her fingers with his mouth and bit them gently, then kissed the imagined hurt away. His sigh conveyed his own satisfaction. Letting her mind drift, Rhea replayed the pleasure of their lovemaking until she stirred with the sudden renewal of her desire.

"Am I too heavy?" Murmuring the question, Hux made to move, but Rhea held him firmly in place.

"No, you're perfect."

Chuckling softly, Hux ruffled the curls that spilled over her forehead. "I was wondering how long it would take you to realize that."

"You do have a way of twisting words to suit yourself, Huxley Benton. Maybe you really are a sneaky snake."

"Snakes aren't sneaky. They warn you before they strike. Remember?"

"Um, well, I guess you can't be a snake anyway."

"Why not?"

She arched a brow as she said, "Snakes are cold-blooded."

"And I'm not, huh?" He touched his lips to hers. Though Hux's kiss was sweet, Rhea felt her heartbeat accelerate and a responding chord was struck where they were still joined. "Can I wrap myself around you anyway, my beautiful goddess? I think you're perfect —for me."

Rhea grew warm at his statement, but couldn't resist continuing the banter. "Oh, so now we're both perfect. I guess that's why we're matched so well." She used that same nail to draw a sensuous circle around his nipple. "In here anyway."

"We'd match well anywhere."

"Um, I'm not so sure about that," Rhea said, suddenly thinking about the trouble they'd had professionally.

"Well, barring public places of course."

"Or working together."

"I think we'd work well together, Rhea, if only you'd give us a chance."

"Now wait a minute," Rhea said, unsuccessfully trying to wiggle out of Hux's embrace. "I'm not the one who . . ."

Hux put his finger over her mouth. "Shush. Let's forget about the past and start over. Okay?"

"No more tricks?"

"W-e-e-ll . . ." Hux said, drawing the word out until Rhea poked him in the ribs. "I promise. Maybe we could start by working on the fashion video idea together."

"I don't know. I've put a lot of work into my presentation. Are you willing to give yours up?"

"Hmm. I've put a lot of work into mine too. Maybe we should submit them both to the executive board on Monday as planned. But if they choose your idea, Rhea, I'll do everything I can to help you execute it."

"Fair enough," Rhea said, warmed by Hux's agreeable attitude. Was it an indication of his feelings for her? If so, perhaps she had found the real man under the glossy exterior. "I know you're terrific at your job. It was the way you tried to trick me into seeing you that put me off. I promise I'll support your idea if it's chosen."

"Great! We'll be partners then."

"Want to shake on it?"

Hux narrowed his eyes. "I can think of a more creative way to seal the deal."

Rhea's sigh was greatly exaggerated. "When you look at me with those electric green eyes of yours, I'm powerless to resist."

"So you like my eyes, huh? Is that why you tempted me with that apple?"

When Rhea nodded solemnly, Hux flipped over on his back, bringing her with him so she straddled his thighs. Rhea gasped as he slid his hands up her belly to her breasts. She realized he was hard inside her.

"Then look into my eyes and follow my instructions explicitly," Hux murmured. "Unless you can think of something more creative, that is."

For some reason, Rhea didn't even want to try.

Following Hux's directions was a very satisfying experience, she soon discovered. Their lovemaking was abandoned, draining the last of her energy. Afterward she lay snuggled in Hux's arms until she slept.

The room was dark when she awoke sometime later. The bed was empty. Where was Hux? The door was closed, but a faint light showed through the space between it and the floor.

"Hux? Are you there?" she called, getting out of bed to investigate.

The door opened and Hux slipped in, the light from the living area burnishing his nude form. "I'm here."

"What were you doing out there?" she asked suspiciously.

"Finding an offering for my voluptuous goddess." From behind his back he produced one of the untouched peaches she'd brought out with the wine. "There are all kinds of delicious things one can do with ripe fruit."

"Like what?" Rhea asked, backing onto the bed.

"Let me show you."

Wide-eyed, she realized Hux was already aroused. "You're insatiable," she murmured as she took the juicy peach from him.

CHAPTER SIX

Sunlight was streaming through the bedroom window when Rhea woke again. No alarm. No reason to get up just yet. Snuggling into her pillow, she inhaled the scent of ripe peaches.

Rhea sat up and inspected the pillow cover. "Peaches?" Then, vividly remembering how peach juice had dripped onto the material, a slow smile lifted the corners of her mouth. "Hux?" she called softly, but there was no answer.

She checked the clock. Quarter past six. Perhaps he was in the kitchen making coffee or scrambling eggs. Though she wasn't an early riser herself, she allowed the fault in others.

Hopping out of bed, Rhea approached the bedroom's wall-length closet. Her sewing machine was tucked away at one end, and a dressmaker's form stood sentinel outside the door, wearing one of her robes. She grabbed the rust-and-magenta garment, covering herself as she glanced into the mirror. After smoothing down her dark-auburn hair with a brush, she headed for the kitchen, an expectant smile on her face. But there her good mood quickly faded.

Hux wasn't busy making breakfast as she'd hoped. He'd left without even saying good-bye.

Why? Rhea wondered, now riddled with doubt about their night together. She'd really allowed herself to get carried away, hadn't she? Wandering back into the living area, she sat on the couch and looked out the window. Had she made a tremendous mistake?

But she'd been so sure . . .

Hux had convinced her . . .

Making love with him had seemed like the natural thing to do in the dark of night, but now, in the harsh clear reality of day, Rhea wondered how she'd lost control so easily. Perhaps if Hux were still by her side, she'd feel differently. But since he hadn't even bothered to kiss her good-bye, who knew what Hux thought about their lovemaking? Was it just a spectacular romp to him or had it meant something deeper? Rhea wondered, not wanting to admit how much Hux could mean to her.

Hadn't she known she wasn't his type right from the start? Had Hux been excited merely by the challenge of seducing her, ready for new conquests now that he'd been successful?

Someone more glamorous.

More pliable.

Thinner.

"Damn it! Don't do this to yourself, Rhea Mitchell!"

Now she was angry with herself. Rhea had long ago decided that "thin" wasn't worth starvation, excruciating headaches, and a drastic change in personality —all of which she'd suffered for many years. And having accepted herself as she was, Rhea was rarely conscious of her size.

Why should she be? She wasn't horribly over-weight—just out of step with what was considered fashionable. Her family had been supportive of her decision to stop aiming for a goal she'd never reach without making unacceptable sacrifices. And she'd never lost out on friends—or boyfriends—because of it.

Not before Huxley Benton, that is!

"Don't start feeling inadequate because of some sexy playboy you don't even like!" she told herself.

But in the end she had liked him, or she never would have gone to bed with Hux, Rhea realized. And that thought made her feel even worse.

"Hey, old man, long time no see!" Hux said, heartily slapping Rafe Damon on the back.

Rafe steadied himself by hanging on to his tripod, and looked at his friend in surprise. "What do you mean, long time? You had dinner, played cards, and spent the night with us—when? A couple of weeks ago?"

"Ah, it's just a figure of speech." Hux couldn't stop grinning. "It's a great day, isn't it?"

"Are you all right, Hux?" The photographer raised a brow and his heavy lids lifted, revealing dark curious eyes, which inspected his friend closely. "It's not quite seven A.M., and unless my memory is faulty, you usually aren't even civil before nine or ten."

"Hey, times change. Things change. People change."

"Whew! I get the feeling this is going to be some

94

discussion when we have the time for it," Rafe said, fixing his Hasselblad camera on the tripod. "But right now we'd better get started before the models have a field day with the Easter display."

"Right," Hux said agreeably, looking around at the screeching kids running through the deserted toy department. "I'll have Irene round up the little monsters."

"Good idea. There's Clarence in his Easter bunny suit now. I still don't know how you managed to convince him to play the part, especially since he had to shave his beard and mustache."

"Money talks, or haven't you heard?" Hux asked in his cynic's voice. "Clarence may prefer to play Santa Claus, but I'm sure he'd like to eat before next December."

Waving to the old actor, who looked decidedly uncomfortable in his fluffy pink-and-white costume, Hux strode off jauntily and found his assistant. After asking Irene to get the kids in order, he allowed himself to think about the most beautiful, warmest, sexiest woman he'd ever had the good fortune to meet.

Too bad he'd had to leave Rhea so early this morning. Warmed by the picture she made snuggled into her pillow, he hadn't had the heart to wake her merely to tell her he had to go because of an early-morning publicity shoot. And twenty minutes ago, when he got to Haldan-Northrop, he'd forced himself away from the phone. Undoubtedly Rhea wasn't even awake yet, but he'd certainly call her later.

Maybe he could see her that night!

Unaccustomed to being so excited about anything,

Hux couldn't get over the fact that his romantic relationship with Rhea affected him in other ways. He seemed to be looking at everything with a fresh eye: the store, his job; even the possibility of being promoted to vice-president met with his approval today.

In the midst of pondering his chances at the promotion, Hux failed to see the kid until it was too late. Hit behind the knees by a short whirlwind, Hux almost fell, only saving himself by grabbing on to a nearby counter.

"Hey . . . !"

"Hey, yourself! Doncha know better than to stand around blocking the aisles?" the small auburn-haired boy muttered, glaring up indignantly at Hux.

"Charlie, where are you?" a woman called. "You know you have to wear makeup whether you like it or not. We're already late. Do you want to lose this job?"

"Oops. Mom!" The kid looked ready to panic. "Stall her, mister, would you?"

Then Charlie was off around the counter to the right. Hux stared after him, grinning, until his mother came up beside him.

"Did you see a boy with dark reddish hair?" the woman asked, panting.

"Um, yes, I did."

"Which way did he go?"

"Which way? Uh, I think it was to the right. Or was it the left?"

"Oh, never mind. I'll find him myself."

When the woman took off in the wrong direction, Hux realized what he'd done. He'd conspired with the kid to lead his mother astray! What had he been

96

thinking? Any delay would cost money. Surprisingly, he couldn't get upset about it.

The morning was full of odd surprises.

Though he consulted with Rafe, then watched the photographer set up and take his shots, Hux barely kept his attention on the goings-on at Haldan-Northrop. His mind kept straying to an apartment paradise and the lush woman he'd left there. He remembered their night together as though every detail had been burned into his brain. Recounting the moments one by one, he got to the incident with the peach when he felt a sharp tug at his sleeve.

"Hux, didn't you hear me? Or are you trying to ignore me?"

"Oh, Melissa," he said with pleasure. As Hux looked down at the golden-haired woman, his eyes gravitated to her stomach, which had grown larger since he'd seen her a couple of weeks before. "I hope you're feeling . . . well."

She seemed oblivious to his discomfort. "Pregnancy does agree with me. But I guess I'm going to have to quit my job sooner than I thought. Even my altered costume won't hide the baby much longer."

Hux cleared his throat. "Is that why you stopped by today, to discuss leaving?"

Her cheek dimpled. "Actually, I thought I'd volunteer to pose as an Easter egg. I've got the right shape for it," she said, lightly patting her stomach.

Looking into her cornflower-blue eyes, filled with laughter, Hux realized she was teasing him. He took a deep breath and grinned at her. "Actually, you'd make a pretty lopsided Easter egg."

"I knew I could find that famous sense of humor if I

tried hard enough. You've got to stop treating me differently just because I'm having a baby. And speaking of which, I have something to ask you."

"Uh-oh. Sounds serious."

"It is. Rafe and I want you to be our baby's godfather."

"Godfather? Me?"

"Yes, you. What do you say? Are you willing to take the little monster on?" she asked, referring to his characteristic sentiment concerning children.

"Uh, but I don't know anything about being a godfather. Why me?"

"Because we think you'd be a great godfather. In spite of the way you malign kids, you've managed to make Hank and Gretta adore you," she said, referring to the children of Rafe's first marriage. "And Rafe and I both love you, Hux. I expect the baby will too."

Feeling a large lump settle in his throat, Hux swallowed hard and tried to act casual. "If you and Rafe are sure . . . I, uh, guess I could find out what a godfather's supposed to do. I hope the little devil can bear with a novice."

Grabbing his jacket lapels, Melissa pulled Hux toward her. On tiptoes she kissed his cheek, then let go and beamed up at him. "Thanks, Hux. If you don't mind, I think I'll see if my husband needs any help."

A godfather! Hux thought, feeling even better than he had earlier—until he realized he might be expected to hold the baby! What if he dropped it? Hux fought the panicky feeling that made him want to call Melissa back and tell her he'd changed his mind.

Maybe Rhea could coach him on how to hold a

baby so he wouldn't do it all wrong. But what if something happened to Rafe and Melissa in the future? As godfather, wouldn't Hux be expected to raise the child as his own? He didn't know the first thing about parenting! What he did know is that he'd never send their child to a series of boarding schools. He'd make sure the kid felt wanted and loved.

Still immersed in the odd daydream, Hux looked over to Melissa and Rafe whispering together, their heads only inches apart. Melissa was beautiful in her pregnancy. She'd be the perfect mother. . . .

Suddenly, the strangest thing happened—Hux started wondering what it would be like to have a child of his own. The odd idea made him think of the previous night and the warmhearted woman with whom he'd spent it. Hux's mouth went dry as he imagined Rhea in a new, appealing role: that of luscious earth mother, his baby in her arms.

Good God, what had come over him? Hux wondered, trying to shake the inveigling thought. He wasn't meant to be a father. Or a husband for that matter. Didn't he have his reputation as a perennial bachelor to consider? Besides, he hardly knew Rhea Mitchell!

Even so, he couldn't rid himself of those strange imaginings, and as the morning progressed he grew more and more distant from the shoot. He kept picturing Rhea as he'd last seen her—in bed, curled up with her pillow—and he imagined himself joining her there. He called Rhea several times, unable to reach her, and then Hux began to feel distinctly out of sorts. The need to talk with her was almost overwhelming.

Where was she?

Who was enjoying her company now?

When would he see her again?

By the time he dialed her number for the seventh time from a phone at the back of the toy department, his patience had almost run out. Maybe he should go back to her building and wait for her. But just as he was about to slam down the receiver, she answered, and a weight lifted from his chest. He was so relieved, Hux hardly noticed Rhea was rather reserved.

"Hi, you sexy woman," he said softly, so as not to be overheard. "I've been thinking about you. And you wouldn't believe what those thoughts are doing to me physically."

Eyes wide, Rhea wondered why Hux would talk to her like this when he'd left her without even saying good-bye. Still piqued, she coolly queried, "Who is this?"

He shouted indignantly, "It's Hux!" Then he lowered his voice. She wondered if he was trying to play on her sympathies when he asked, "How could you not recognize the man to whom you made such passionate love last night?" Was his hurt tone practiced?

"Sorry."

"I forgive you," he said indulgently, making the fine hairs rise on the back of Rhea's neck. "Just don't let it happen again."

"Was there something important you wanted to discuss?" Since she'd decided to proceed with caution where he was concerned, Rhea purposely kept her voice neutral. "I'm very busy today. I have an appointment in less than an hour."

"You have a date?"

"A client."

"But The Hidden Woman won't move to Haldan-Northrop for several more weeks."

"But I still have a business to run if I don't want to lose my customers during the transition."

Before he could reply, she heard a woman's voice in the background calling, "Hux, can you come over here right away? I need you desperately."

Rhea was shocked. Was the playboy actually calling her when he was with another woman?

"Just a second. I'll be right there," he yelled back, then returned to his conversation with Rhea. "Uh, what about tonight?"

Was he going to suggest another assignation? Hadn't he gone straight from her bed to some other —probably more glamorous and thinner—woman? She wouldn't have credited Hux with *that* much callousness. And now he wanted to come back to her. Was he so sexually driven that he was anxious to take *her* to bed again? Rhea turned her anger away from herself and aimed it at him. If he even dared suggest . . . !

"Rhea, are you there?"

"What about tonight?" she choked out.

"I'd like to see you." Once more he lowered his voice. "I'm sorry I decided to be noble and let you sleep while I went off to work. Maybe not kissing you good-bye is what's been distracting me all morning. But then again, if I'd kissed you I might have been late."

"You're . . . at the store?"

"Yeah. I've been here since six thirty this morn-

101

ing," he said, making Rhea feel foolish for her suspicions. "I wish I were with you instead. Right now we could be together, walking hand-in-hand through Central Park."

Wondering what had made her jump to conclusions, Rhea absently said, "You want to stroll through the park in this weather?"

"So it's a little chilly. I'm sure we could find ways to keep each other warm. Even if there were six-foot drifts of snow, it would seem like a paradise if you were with me," Hux told her softly, making Rhea's stomach flutter. "Listen, Irene is waving at me frantically. I've got to take care of some problem. About tonight . . . ?"

"I can meet you somewhere later."

"The Russian Tea Room at seven?"

"I'll be there."

Hanging up, Rhea walked to her window and looked down at Central Park. Cold February winds whipped through the barren trees, and patches of white covered part of the ground. Paradise, huh? Well, maybe it would be with Hux by her side.

Rhea was somewhat appalled at the way she'd jumped to the wrong conclusions about the man. Hux hadn't regretted being with her, nor had he gone on to another woman as she'd supposed. Why had she given herself such a hard time? Was she really that insecure? That in itself was an odd feeling, one she'd never experienced with any other man.

Was that fact significant?

Did it make Hux special?

Now there was a scary thought. Even though she'd decided she liked Hux—even though she'd made love with him—Rhea still didn't think they were right for each other. She was convinced it was merely a matter of time before he realized that she didn't fit in with his life-style and had no desire to. She might appeal to him for the moment, but undoubtedly he would eventually tire of her uniqueness and drift back to the familiar.

But even knowing that, Rhea couldn't help wanting to see Hux anyway. After all, what if she were wrong again?

She'd simply have to be extra careful so she wouldn't get hurt. She could enjoy being with Huxley Benton without getting herself in deeper emotionally. She'd have to make sure they took things slower, at least for a while.

She decided she couldn't let the evening end in bed again, and coming to that conclusion, Rhea became irritated with her own logic.

Later, after she and Hux had shared a romantic dinner at the Russian Tea Room, Rhea wondered why she'd ever made such a ridiculous promise to herself. Hux had been charming and attentive—the perfect date. Now, walking with him, all she could think about was the ecstasy they'd shared in each other's arms the night before and how deprived she was going to feel when she told Hux he couldn't stay.

"Cold?" he asked as they crossed Fifty-seventh Street.

"A little. But the walk will warm me up."

"I can do the job faster and more pleasantly."

Stopping suddenly, Hux wrapped his arms around Rhea and kissed her with an unrestrained passion

103

that took her by surprise. Remembering her good intentions, she was hesitant about returning the embrace. But what could happen on a midtown Manhattan sidewalk? She kissed Hux longingly, sliding her tongue along his, slipping her hands inside his unbuttoned wool overcoat and around to his back.

Hux groaned as he pulled Rhea snuggly against him and ran his tongue along the shell of her ear. The sensation was so exquisite she forgot to breathe.

"A taxi would get us to your apartment so much faster," he whispered, his tone suggestive. "Are you sure you want to walk home?"

Rhea gulped and sucked in the cold night air. Taking things slowly was not going to be easy. "After eating caviar, blini, shashlik, and strawberries Romanoff? You bet I want to walk," she said lightly, using the filling meal as an excuse. "Haven't you heard, 'Past the lips, straight to the hips'?"

"Who cares? I've decided I prefer full-hipped women," Hux murmured, sliding his hands down Rhea's body to stroke her hips sensually.

"Hux!" she whispered, desperately trying to stop his moving hands. "Thanks for the compliment, but we must be going."

"All right." Hux sighed dramatically. "And if burning off those decadent Russian calories will make you happy, I guess we'll walk."

Her excuse for avoiding the intimacy of a taxi's backseat had worked, but what excuse could she use when they arrived at her apartment? Undoubtedly he would expect to stay the night. Saying no might be enough to make Hux leave for good and that angered Rhea.

Realizing she was jumping to conclusions again, Rhea told herself to calm down. Hux might be happy to have an excuse to leave. That thought made her frown. The idea that he might want to go home didn't sit any better with her than his possibly assuming he'd be able to stay. What in the world was wrong with her? She couldn't seem to make up her mind what she wanted or how she expected Hux to act.

Thank goodness they were walking. The cold night air might clear her muddled mind. Surprisingly enough, she found herself relaxing as Hux asked her about her business.

"Did you feel you were taking a big risk when you started The Hidden Woman?"

"Not really. At least I didn't see it that way. I had a lot of contacts through my modeling career, and I worked at both jobs for a while. When I decided to concentrate on fashion consulting, I knew I'd have to pinch pennies until The Hidden Woman got going. But the challenge made it worth the temporary poverty."

Hux nodded in agreement. "Work can get pretty boring unless the challenges keep getting greater."

"I guess that's one of the reasons I agreed to move my business to Haldan-Northrop."

"It's time for me to make a change in my career also. I've thought about starting my own promotions firm, but the idea doesn't really appeal to me, at least not right now. In a couple of weeks Haldan-Northrop will have an opening for a new vice-president of promotions, advertising, and public relations. I've decided I want that job no matter *what* I have to do to get it."

105

"You certainly sound determined. Do you always get what you want?"

Despite the light of only a streetlamp, Rhea was sure she saw a challenge issue from Hux's sparkling eyes. He said, "Often enough."

Then he slipped his arm around her and pulled her against him without slowing his pace. Had he still been talking about business or had he been referring to his personal relationships?

A few minutes later they arrived at her building. By the time they entered the elevator, Rhea was quite nervous once more. But it seemed Hux wasn't as anxious to get close to her in the elevator as he had been the night before. Or was it that he was more confident of what would happen once inside her apartment?

When they were in her living area and she was in the act of hanging up her coat, Hux teasingly said, "Ah, paradise."

Rhea froze, then quickly choked out, "Paradise isn't always what it seems." Closing the closet door, she turned smack into Hux. His arms immediately wound around her. She knew she'd better tell him he'd have to leave now, before it was too late. "In addition to snakes, there are lots of other pitfalls."

"Don't worry, I won't fall into any pit. I've got my moves down pat, or hadn't you noticed?" Hux asked with a grin. "Besides, paradise isn't a place. It's a state of mind."

Hux lowered his head to kiss her, and for all her good intentions Rhea couldn't stop him. It seemed so right and natural to be in his arms, to feel his mouth move over hers, his lips nudge hers open, his tongue exploring and dueling with her own. The sensations he created were so exciting they took her breath away. It must have been an eternity before he ended the kiss and she took in a great gulp of air.

"See what I mean?"

"Ah, Hux," Rhea began, trying to wiggle out of his grasp, to give herself some breathing room. He held her fast, not giving an inch, so she contented herself with propping her hands flat against his chest. "I've given what happened last night some thought and . . ."

"And?" he echoed before kissing her again.

Rhea's knees grew weak as she responded to this next passionate embrace with a fervor hardly indicative of a woman who meant to proceed cautiously. When Hux pressed himself against her, her body flamed and Rhea's imagination hopped, skipped, and jumped into the bed in the next room.

What was coming over her? Rhea wondered as she finally succeeded in pulling free, gasping. "*And . . . I realized we moved too fast.*"

Hux scowled at her, his forehead wrinkled over suddenly cautious green eyes. "Are you saying you're sorry we made love?"

"Uh, not exactly. It's just that I, uh, am not comfortable being a man's sparring partner one moment and his lover the next." Rhea looked away from Hux's intense gaze. "The whole thing took me by surprise," she mumbled.

"So what is it you want? To go back to being friendly adversaries?"

"No!" Her response was so vehement Rhea was afraid Hux might guess how vulnerable he could

107

make her. "I merely think we should know one another a lot better before we . . . are . . . think about being intimate."

"I think we've gotten to know each other pretty well in the past few weeks."

His expression was warm and understanding until she added, "That's the problem, Hux. Even though I do like you and feel desperately attracted to you, I recognize that our life-styles are nothing alike." And she'd never be comfortable in his fast lane. But seeing how his eyes had shuttered, Rhea couldn't tell him that. "I merely think a man and a woman should have more in common than physical attraction."

Hux seemed thoughtful, but not angry or rejecting. Rhea was both delighted and distraught when he asked, "Then how about spending tomorrow together? We can get to know one another better over brunch. And maybe visit a few galleries."

"Oh, I can't. My family is having a party tomorrow."

"Do you have to go?"

Since it was a party celebrating her thirty-fourth birthday, she did. "I not only have to go, I want to." Hux looked so disappointed—mirroring the way she felt—that Rhea impulsively suggested, "But why don't you come with me? My parents wouldn't mind."

"You mean it?" The green eyes seemed to sparkle with pleasure. "I'd love to meet your family."

"Terrific. Can you be here at two?"

"I'll be here whenever you want me," he said softly, and Rhea felt there was a wealth of meaning behind those simple words.

She only hoped that Hux wouldn't regret attending one of her family's unsophisticated get-togethers. It wouldn't exactly be the kind of event that appealed to a playboy. Wondering if she should warn him it was her birthday, Rhea decided against it. He'd probably feel obligated to bring a present, and she didn't want him to.

"Can I have one last kiss before I go?"

Rhea nodded and felt her pulse jump. But she was disappointed when Hux gave her an almost chaste kiss. And closing the door behind him, she tried to deny she was a little disappointed that he hadn't at least *tried* to overcome her objections to continuing their intimate relationship.

CHAPTER SEVEN

"Happy birthday to you! Happy birthday to you!" sang the group of thirty or more people gathered around the table in the dining room of the Mitchell family's large, rambling house.

Standing in a corner of the room, Hux silently mouthed the words to the traditional song—he had never prided himself on his singing. As he watched Rhea blow out the candles on her huge birthday cake, he once again wished she'd informed him of the nature of this special occasion before they were on their way out to Queens.

If he had brought a gift for her, he would have felt a little more comfortable. As it was, Hux had been standing around with his hands in his pockets all evening, not knowing what to do or say. Years of excelling at cocktail party banter and business talk had not prepared him for a traditional family party that included elderly aunts, friendly neighbors, and little kids.

Wearing a pin-striped designer suit and dark silk tie while everyone else was dressed casually, Hux knew he stood out like a sore thumb. Although many of Rhea's relatives had gone out of their way to be gracious toward him, Hux was uneasy with their friendly, sometimes overly familiar questions, not knowing quite how to respond.

And there were so many people it was impossible to remember every name. Scanning the gathering, Hux tested his memory. The ancient white-haired ladies over there were her great-aunts Elsa and Magda, he was pretty sure. They were the ones who'd asked if he was a movie star. Then the woman with the dyed-red hair—wasn't that Aunt Ginger, who was thrice-divorced and searching for husband number four? She'd looked Hux up and down speculatively.

The rest of the faces blurred before him. Hux knew he'd do well to remember the names of Rhea's parents and two sisters. He focused on the immediate family again, at the table where Rhea was tackling a pile of cards and gifts.

"Open this one," urged Rhea's older sister, Gaye, handing her a brightly wrapped package.

"No, she's supposed to read the cards first," said Stuart Mitchell, Rhea's father. "Opening the packages before the cards is backwards."

"Why? Who says so, Dad?" argued Gaye good-naturedly. "Is that the law according to Emily Post?"

"He doesn't read Emily Post," asserted Leonora, Rhea's mother, a plump pretty woman in her late fifties.

"Hey, who says I don't read her? This is an intelligent family," insisted Stuart, adjusting the frames of his bifocals. "How do you think we ended up with such a successful daughter, er, daughters," he amended, glancing apologetically at Gaye and his

111

youngest daughter, Diana, a tall woman in her late twenties.

"Open the packages first, Rhea," demanded Gaye.

"Oh, relax, everybody," said Rhea with a low throaty laugh. "It's my birthday. Shouldn't I get to choose how I go about this?"

"That's telling them," broke in Diana, her eyes sparkling mischievously. "Don't listen to this argumentative bunch or we'll be here all night."

Hux silently agreed, relieved that they weren't going to take a vote. Then someone poked him in the arm. Startled, he looked down to see Rhea's grandfather, eighty-two-year-old Edgar Boviak, staring up at him. The white-haired, rather stooped old man grinned and poked him again with his cane.

"You want my attention, Mr. Boviak?" Hux asked drily. "I'm listening."

"Good," said Grandpa Boviak. "I hope you're taking all of this in. We've got a nice family here. And Rhea's real spirited, hard-working, honest, and healthy as a horse."

"I'm impressed," Hux admitted, wondering if the old man was going to suggest he check Rhea's teeth.

"Why, this family has lived here in Queens almost four generations now. You know my own father came over from Europe, don't you?" When Hux nodded, the elderly man went on. "And we're all proud of Rhea and what she's accomplished. Not to say there's anything wrong with Gaye marrying and keeping house or Diana's going into her father's hardware business. But Rhea's the only member of the family to make her own way in Manhattan, to support herself there."

"You can certainly be proud of your granddaughter." Returning his gaze to Rhea, Hux watched her chat with the noisy group as she opened her presents. Removing a pair of antique goblets from one of the gift boxes, she read the accompanying crayon-colored, child-created cards. Then she hugged the donors—Gaye and her husband and their two small children.

"So," Grandpa Boviak continued, "what I mean to say is that everybody stands behind their kin in this family. There isn't any place too far or any trouble too big for us to go and help them, even if we have to travel to Manhattan. If we can stop troubles beforehand, we'll do that too. So, as the head of this family, I'd like to know about your intentions."

"Intentions?"

"What are your intentions toward Rhea? Are you planning on marrying my little beauty?"

Taken aback, Hux stared down into the man's sharp, old eyes. Rhea's grandfather was serious and he certainly wasn't senile. Was he asking this embarrassing question because doing so was traditional for his generation? Or had Rhea said something about their relationship to her family? Had she hinted he was important to her? Hux cleared his throat.

"We haven't gotten to the point of discussing marriage yet, Mr. Boviak."

"Call me Grandpa Boviak. Everybody else does."

"Uh, sure." Hux straightened his tie and wondered how long it would take for Rhea to unwrap all the packages. He almost jumped as he received another sharp jab.

"Anyhow, I wanted to get things straight," said

Grandpa. "You look like a good-tempered young man and you must make enough money, considering you're wearing a decent suit. I just want you to know I stand behind my granddaughter. You'd better not hurt that girl or you'll have me to answer to."

"You don't have to worry," Hux assured him, realizing he was telling the frail old man the truth. "My intentions are quite honorable."

"Keep them as good as your looks, boy." Chuckling, Grandpa moved away slowly, using his cane. Hux heard him muttering to himself, "Handsome young devil. Reminds me of myself at his age."

Seeing guests now circling the table, helping themselves to refreshments, Hux was relieved Rhea had finally finished with her presents. Pausing at the task of cutting the cake, Rhea raised her head and caught his eye. Full lips curving into a smile, she brought a piece of the cake and a cup of punch over to him.

"Would you like some? I'm sorry I've been busy so long. Whenever we have a birthday party, the celebrant has to be the center of attraction, you know."

"That's to be expected," said Hux, accepting the food. "I only wish you'd told me it was your birthday sooner. I would have gotten you a gift."

"I didn't want to tell you about my birthday because I thought you might feel obligated." Two spots of color suddenly bloomed on Rhea's cheeks. "After all, we haven't known each other very long."

Why was she embarrassed? Hux wondered. Was it because of the intense way they'd "known" each other a couple of nights ago? Didn't she think that qualified her for a little special attention from him?

And considering his conversation with her grandfather, she must have said something to her family about him.

"As usual I got more gifts than I can possibly use. Do you know my mother crocheted me an afghan? And Aunt Augusta gave me one of her miniature paintings?" Rhea beamed with pleasure.

As he ate his cake and followed Rhea into the living room, Hux saw a few of the younger guests rolling back the rug so they could dance. In the area by the open stairway someone was organizing a game of charades.

What an elaborate celebration the Mitchells were having—for an adult. The last birthday party Hux had attended was an ice-cream and pin-the-tail-on-the-donkey affair for his friend Rafe's little daughter.

And before that . . . all of a sudden Hux was reminded of the year he was ten, when his mother invited all the prissy little kids from his new private school for cake and milk. What a time that was! Everyone had to sit around politely and all the little girls had to keep their expensive dresses clean. It had been quite boring—Hux hadn't known anyone very well—and he'd told his mother he never wanted a birthday party again. She'd been happy to comply.

"Want to dance?" Rhea asked, interrupting his reverie.

"Sure," Hux said, turning his attention back to her. "But there's no music."

"I'm aware of that. I meant do you want to dance as soon as they find some records to play. I thought I should get your attention first. You looked so . . . unamused."

"Really? I'm sorry. I was lost in thought, that's all. Does your family always have this kind of get-together for birthdays?"

"Yes, and they also celebrate anniversaries, graduations, holidays, and anything else they can think of."

"Must keep everyone busy."

He thought Rhea looked pensive for a few minutes, but she quickly regained her vivaciousness as some old records were brought out and put on the Mitchell's stereo. The first dance was a polka of all things, probably the only kind of dance Hux didn't know. Hopping gracefully from one foot to the other, he thought he was doing a fairly good job of improvisation until he caught Rhea trying to hide a smirk.

"Hey, do you want to hurt my pride?" he asked indignantly. "This is the first time I've ever danced a polka."

"Would you let me give you a lesson? What you're doing resembles an ethnic version of disco."

"Maybe I'm trying to be creative. What's wrong with that?" Despite his remark, Hux watched good-naturedly as Rhea demonstrated some steps. Then he followed her instructions.

They were soon swinging easily around the floor, Rhea's flowing, cinnamon-colored dress and auburn curls fluttering with their movement. She commented, "You learn fast."

"I'm a quick study, especially under duress."

"You think I would resort to force to get you to do the polka correctly?"

"No, but your grandfather warned me to keep you happy—or else. He even beat me a little with his cane."

"Come on."

"Seriously, he asked me about my intentions toward you."

She pulled back to gaze at him in surprise. "You're kidding, aren't you?" When she saw he wasn't, she went on. "How embarrassing! Grandpa always told me he was going to do that, but I never thought he would. Please excuse him."

"No problem. It didn't bother me. The old man probably thought he was doing his duty."

Hux felt oddly disappointed. He'd thought for sure that mentioning Grandpa would get Rhea to jokingly admit she'd told her family Hux was special. But now he wondered if she'd told them anything. Could he think of a clever way to find out? Moving her to the edge of the makeshift dance floor, he slowed down for a more involved conversation.

But there were others present who had dibs on Rhea's time.

"Look who's here!" Gaye called to her sister excitedly.

"Ted! Jackie!" cried Rhea. Hux reluctantly released her so she could greet the strangers. After quickly introducing everyone, Rhea began reminiscing with the new guests and various relatives about old times. Having little to say in such a situation, Hux separated himself from the group.

Obviously thinking he needed to be reassured, Gaye stepped back also. She quietly explained, "Ted and his wife are old friends of ours. A long time ago Rhea and Ted used to go out, then they parted amicably. After that, Ted married Jackie and brought her

117

to meet us. The family always sends them invitations, although they haven't been here in a long time."

"You all invite old boyfriends to family functions?" asked Hux with surprise.

"Sure. Why lose a good friend just because you've stopped dating? We all feel we're part of an even larger family that transcends bloodlines. So we have an open-invitation policy for all our old friends on holidays and special occasions."

Before Hux could respond, Gaye left to answer a call from her small daughter. He looked around the room and noticed Rhea's parents in the middle of the dance floor doing a rousing version of the polka, while nearby great-aunts Elsa and Magda danced together less strenuously. In the hallway Diana and her boyfriend had joined the charades group and were trying to guess what turbaned Aunt Augusta was trying to say with her wild arm motions. What a family!

Hux couldn't help but contrast the gregarious, fun-loving Mitchell clan with his own. His parents would never think of extending a casual, ongoing invitation to their children's friends or even to relatives. The roster for every party or other social gathering hosted by the Bentons was carefully weighed and planned. They cared more for appearances than for sentimental traditions, and Hux often suspected they were gracious only so no one could accuse them of bad manners.

At least that's the way it had always seemed to him. Wasn't his parents' concern for appearances the only reason they still bothered with him at all? Hux knew their lack of warmth was the reason he'd developed into the kind of man he was.

His parents had never been supportive of him, while Rhea's family was openly proud of her accomplishments. No wonder she was so popular and confident. Hux had had to learn to use charm and wit to get the attention his family hadn't given him.

Hux couldn't help feeling left out and a little envious. Did Rhea realize he didn't fit in? That he was lacking? She had something he'd always wanted and had rarely possessed—a real sense of belonging with family and friends.

Expelling his breath with a sound suspiciously close to a sigh, Hux wandered toward the dining room to see if he could find anything stronger than punch to drink. A good shot would surely buoy his spirits.

There were no liquor bottles on the table, but Hux found a decanter of Scotch on the buffet. He poured a couple of ounces into a glass and went to the kitchen to add water and ice. Then he leaned against the counter, sipping it slowly, giving himself a pep talk.

For a person with his background, he was doing fairly well, wasn't he? At least he was conscious of the origin of his life's dissatisfying patterns. Emotionally distant parents had caused Hux to feel he'd never belong. And if he understood the patterns, he could change them, couldn't he? Hadn't that been the reason he'd sought out an old and real friend like Rafe Damon, making it a point to see him and his family as frequently as possible in the past year? Now Hux was going to become the godfather to the Damons' new baby. That would certainly be a commitment—a long-term change for him.

Warmed by the thought, Hux smiled and placed his empty glass on the counter. Rafe and Melissa had confidence in him. And just because he'd felt a little out of his depth tonight at Rhea's family affair didn't mean he couldn't learn to handle such things. Besides, part of his discomfort this evening had been caused by his intense desire to make a good impression.

Rhea would surely understand that. She was a caring and accepting woman. Almost his opposite in some ways, she was also everything he now admitted was important to him. That's why his attraction to her had grown at such a rapid pace. That's why he'd fallen in love.

Love?

The loaded word caused Hux to stand up straight suddenly. It made him want to head back to the dining room to get an even larger dose of scotch.

Love?

Good Lord! He was in love with Rhea!

Slowly realizing the ramifications of his self-disclosure, Hux wondered what he should do now. Go to the woman and tell her how he felt? What if she didn't love him in return? Was there some way he could ascertain her feelings for him?

Feverishly trying to remember Rhea's every remark and action of the past few days, Hux immediately had some serious misgivings. Hadn't Rhea always harped on their differences? Hadn't she said something negative about their dissimilar backgrounds last night? Why had she accused him of appearing "unamused" today? Had she known he was uncomfortable? Could she love a man who didn't immediately fit in with her family?

Pacing the kitchen floor, he battled his doubts. Although rich in friends and family, Rhea had no special man in her life. Were there ways he could convince her she needed one—and more importantly, that he was the one? Surely Rhea would recognize there could be no one more appreciative of her, or more passionately loving. Hux simply had to make her aware of how much she wanted him. . . .

Striding to the doorway, he stopped short, almost colliding with a soft, cinnamon-clad female body.

"Rhea!"

"Are you feeling okay?" she asked, a concerned expression on her face.

"I feel fine. I . . . merely came in here to have a drink."

"Oh, are you tired of all the blather? I know family gatherings aren't the most entertaining events in the world."

"I was entertained," he asserted, reaching out to gather her into his arms. As he nestled her sensuously into his firm length, her lips seemed to part of their own accord. The amber eyes grew hazy. Warmth spread through him as he appreciated the effect he could have on her. He nibbled gently at her lips. "Of course, I can think of many other kinds of entertainment. Want to head back to Manhattan?"

As Rhea entered her apartment nearly an hour later, it was all she could do to keep from leading Hux to the bedroom. During the ride back to Manhattan, cramped in his low-slung gold Porsche, Rhea had been only too physically aware of the sexy man beside her and of the mischievous hand exploring her thigh to the point of sexual arousal.

But now she had to keep her wits about her. After the obvious boredom Hux had displayed at her birthday party, she couldn't expect him to be around for long. Eventually he'd forgo her company for his more sophisticated life in the city's fast lane. It's only a matter of time before he would, Rhea thought, even as his clever hand caressed her hip through the soft jersey of her dress.

"Hux," Rhea breathed as he pressed her against the inside of the door.

"Yes? What would you like, Rhea? Name it. I'll do anything."

"I'd like to have a cool drink and sit down."

"I can't believe that's what you really want. That's not what your eyes are telling me. They look like molten gems—heated by your flaming passions."

"Hux, please," she remonstrated, managing to extricate herself from the strong arms that had held her prisoner. "Those flames have made me very thirsty."

She darted for the kitchen's swinging doors, and the refrigerator. She hoped the frigid air would cool the heat raging in her veins.

"Wherever the lady leads me, I'll follow," he murmured softly, slipping through the doors and heading toward her.

"No! Stay there!" She held up a hand to warn him away. Only distance was going to calm her pulse.

Hux's jungle-green eyes looked positively steamy as he pretended to sulk. "How long am I supposed to stay away from you?"

"Um, how about long enough to have a drink?" Rhea turned to stare into the refrigerator. "Would you like wine, soda, or beer?"

"I'd rather have you . . . and maybe a juicy peach."

Almost banging her head on the refrigerator, she steadied her voice and asked, "You'd like fruit? How about some orange juice?" She pulled out a container and showed it to him. "I can pour you a glass."

"Aw, I have to drink it from a glass? That's no fun." Then, taking heed of her admonishing look, Hux said, "In that case, I guess I'll have to settle for Scotch and water."

"Right. Scotch with lots and lots of water," she mumbled, wishing she could stick Hux in a cold shower. She replaced the juice, took out a bottle of wine, and heaped some ice in a couple of tumblers. Then she opened a cupboard to find the Scotch.

"Pour yourself a good shot too. It'll relax you."

"I'd relax a lot more if you wouldn't stand so close."

"But I want to give you a special gift for your birthday—something pleasurable. Why not accept? I know you'll find it exciting . . . and romantic."

Imagining what he had in mind, Rhea said, "I've had enough excitement for one evening—and one weekend. Why not save your specialty for another time?"

He looked disappointed, and she had to admit she was disappointed too. Why not accept the offer? she thought as she mixed the drinks. Why not accept what Hux was willing to give her? She might want more later, but memories would probably be all she'd have of him.

"Here," she said, handing him a glass and carefully sidling by his tall form. "Let's go sit in the living room. I'll put on some relaxing music."

Kicking her shoes off on the Oriental rug, she went to the stereo and started the record already on the turntable—a jazzy rendition of Near Eastern music she'd thought of suggesting for the soundtrack of her fashion video.

Hux watched her, obviously expecting her to select a seat where he could arrange himself next to her. Soft, pulsating rhythms drifting through the room, she instead wedged herself into a safely narrow chair, avoiding the dangerous open spaces of the chocolate couch. He had no choice but to sit separately, the distance between her chair and his place on the couch an annoying few feet.

Having removed his suit jacket, he took a swig of Scotch. His gaze raked the length of her legs. "Hmm. Is this really all you want tonight? A drink and some small talk? I always thought I could give more than that to the woman I loved."

"What did you say?" she asked, startled.

Hux wore an odd expression. "I, uh—I mean is small talk all I can give to the woman I'd like to be loving?" He reached over to caress her arm.

"Oh." Rhea realized Hux was embarrassed at his original, inexact phrasing. For a minute she'd actually thought he meant he loved her. "I've already told you I think it would be best to slow our relationship a little."

"It's been at least forty-odd hours since Friday night. How slow do we have to go?"

"Slow enough to learn about other things we might

124

have in common. Zooming along at a hundred and fifty miles an hour makes my engine overheat."

"Poor darling!" he exclaimed jokingly. "Your engine is overheating? Let old Hux look under your hood."

"Forget it. It's locked with an antitheft device."

"How alarming!" Hux laughed. "I love your humor. See? That's something we have in common. Now, why don't you come over here?" He patted the couch beside him. "And we'll explore some of our other interests. Tonight is your birthday and I know you want me."

"But I also want us to enjoy the more platonic side of companionship," Rhea insisted, realizing Hux was becoming impossible! "Why can't we just talk? There's a lot you haven't told me."

"Like what?"

She thought quickly. "Well, about the party—how did you like the cake my mother baked for my birthday?"

"It was very good, almost as sweet as me." Loosening his dark-green silk tie, he removed it and then unfastened the top buttons of his shirt, all the while transfixing her with intense, hooded eyes. "Want a taste?"

"One dessert per evening is my rule," she replied, nervously sipping at her drink. "And please keep the rest of your clothes on. About my party, um . . . did any of my relatives, besides Grandpa, talk to you while I was busy opening my presents? I hope someone else tried to make you feel at home."

"Everyone was very gracious, but I'd rather feel at

125

home right here. Can I take off my shoes? Or are they part of the clothing I'm not supposed to remove?"

"That depends on how long you're planning to stay. We have that meeting tomorrow . . ."

"Tomorrow is hours away," he interrupted, slipping his shoes off. "In the meantime I'll be happy to hang around and help you fully savor this evening."

"You don't have to put yourself out," she said, suddenly alarmed at the zinging of her pulse. It actually seemed to dance with the exotic, sensual cadence of the music on the stereo. Why hadn't she thought to play something less atmospheric?

Hux told her, "Well, I'm willing to extend myself . . . if that's what it takes to get you to accept my birthday gift."

"It would be more special at another time."

"Oh, come on. Your heart is telling you I'm special all the time—if you'd only listen. Can't you be open about your feelings?"

"I am being open," she objected.

"But we could open you a little farther."

Fascinated, she watched him undo the rest of his shirt buttons, baring his tanned chest to the waist. Staring at the newly revealed surface covered lightly with golden hair, she let her gaze fall lower. One of his hands rested below his belt and Rhea waited breathlessly to see if he would undress further. Her eyes widened as she glanced away. A strong wave of desire coursed through her, making her gulp her drink down the wrong way. She coughed hard and uncontrollably, tears springing to her eyes.

Hux rose immediately to kneel by her side, patting her on the back. "Are you all right?" he asked, brows furrowed, concern tightening his voice. "Did you choke on a piece of ice?" She gasped out a quick negative, starting to catch her breath, and he looked relieved. Then he teased, "Maybe I should apply mouth-to-mouth resuscitation anyway. Just to be safe."

Rhea wiped her eyes and laughed. Only Hux would use a coughing fit to try and seduce her. And the offer was so tempting. . . .

He continued, "Let me make you feel better."

"That would work for the moment maybe, but I don't know about later on," she demurred, thinking how easy it would be to get deeply and dangerously involved with him.

"You think I don't have lasting value? Why, beneath this expensive-looking veneer is something even more precious—pure gold. How long is it going to take you to appreciate my personal combination of special charm, special intelligence, special humor, and, especially, overwhelming sexiness?"

"Add special *conceit* to that list."

Hux laughed good-naturedly.

Rhea couldn't escape the tantalizing aroma of him —cologne mixed with his body's own tempting, musky scent. As his hands moved down her back to the curve of her hips, warmth radiated through her. Was it really necessary to resist his enticing offer?

"You're definitely special," she told him shakily. "I guess it wouldn't hurt to accept . . . one kiss from you for my birthday."

Placing her hands on either side of his finely chiseled face, Rhea explored his warm mouth with a

127

lingering kiss. Her heart beat rapidly as she leaned forward, savoring each nuance of his searching lips.

The intense sensations spiraling out from her center told her how much she wanted him. Should she indulge her desires and ignore her fears? Hux was like no other man she'd ever known. He made her feel things she'd never felt with anyone else.

Couldn't she be wrong about his quickly tiring of her? Why should she assume he would when he seemed so enamored of her? Running the fingers of one hand through his hair, she increased the pressure of her embrace and gently bit his lower lip.

Hux made a murmuring sound and pulled away.

"What's the matter?" she asked.

"You said you only wanted one kiss from me."

"So? I wasn't finished with it."

"My dear lovely but naughty and greedy goddess. You finished the first kiss and were taking two more."

"I was not!"

"Why is it so hard to admit? You want a lot more from me than kisses and hugs, Rhea. Every move you make with your body proves it."

"Maybe I'm just practicing a new dance," she said, "to this exotic music."

Closing her eyes, Rhea concentrated on the melody, which conjured up the image of a mysterious, dark-veiled seductress dancing in a jungle glade. Stepping lightly, the figure twisted and whirled like a flame around her chosen man.

As if he were aware of her fantasy, Hux whispered, "How about practicing the dance of love?"

Rhea tried not to squirm as she realized he'd managed to slip his hands under her skirt and was now stroking the nylon-covered flesh of her thighs. When his fingers brushed the tender spots inside and above her knees, the warmth she'd been feeling blazed into fire.

"Don't you want me?" he asked in a provocative whisper. "Why won't you tell me? Better yet, show me how much."

"Umm, want to kiss you," she murmured, words slurred by passion. Why was he so insistent about her admitting her desire for him? Was her answer so important? Did his demand mean that he cared?

Catching her as she slid off the chair to her knees, he pressed her tightly to him. She wound her arms about his neck and took the slightly parted lips he offered. They tasted unbearably sweet. Her tongue meeting his in an erotic duet, their very breaths melding, Rhea felt the flames within her grow higher. The mysterious woman in her imagination removed her robe, her dark veil—and Rhea saw herself in a flowing skirt and halter of red. As she twirled around her lover, her path became a fiery haze. Rhea sensuously moved her hips.

Hux's tight embrace loosened as once more he broke their kiss. "Hux!"

"What's wrong, Rhea?"

"Why are you acting so strangely? You keep leading me on and then running away."

"I'm just giving you room, darling. You need to remove my clothes. You're supposed to unwrap birthday presents, aren't you?"

Appeased, she couldn't resist. Just as she'd removed her veil in her imagination, Rhea threw away caution. Reaching out with trembling hands, she slipped the shirt off his shoulders and unfastened his belt. Opening the zipper of his pants, her fingers brushed the heat of his growing tumescence, making him flinch and exhale sharply. She hesitated.

He cupped her palm and fingers, carefully guiding her hand over his arousal. "For you, Rhea."

Quickly pulling down the back zipper of her dress, he pushed the garment down over her shoulders and waist, exposing her sheer, ivory-colored undergarments. Her nipples swelled. They pressed tightly against the lacy material of her bra.

"I want to pay homage to my beautiful goddess," he murmured, cupping her breasts, kissing a ripening bud through its fragile covering.

"Wait a minute. I'm supposed to do the exploring here," she complained breathlessly. "It's my birthday and you're the present."

"Are you finally admitting you want me?"

"Yes, Hux. Just as you've always known." Gently she tugged at his briefs and pants, drawing them down over his narrow hips, revealing him rigid and ready for her.

She caught her breath. Taking advantage of the momentary pause, he unhooked her bra and captured a nipple with his mouth, drawing gently at it. Achingly sweet sensations blossomed out from Rhea's incandescent core. The dancing woman in her mind stripped off her red garments to uncover the pale flame of heated flesh beneath, just as Hux uncovered her own deepest passion.

"Tell me you want me."

"I want you. . . . I want to make love with you . . . now."

"So you're finally ready to receive my offering, goddess?"

Quickly stripping off the rest of their clothes, he lay down beside her—naked and fully aroused. Rhea swept her hands over his proud tanned body, reveling in his skin's delicious texture. Rubbing herself against him, she was gratified to hear him groan with pleasure. His bold fingers moved over her breasts and belly until they slipped lower, between her legs.

Almost crying out at his touch, Rhea nevertheless welcomed his tender exploration. Parting her thighs, she let the exquisite sensations take her farther and farther. Trying to come back then, before reaching the point of no return, she gazed into his smokey eyes.

"Wait," she insisted, rising to a sitting position.

"Oh, but I've been waiting for your love . . . your loving a long time."

He'd mentioned the word love again! Did Hux actually want her love? Rhea wondered as her heart did a double flip-flop. Would she, in turn, ever receive that elusive emotion from him?

She leaned over to kiss him tenderly. "You don't have to wait any longer."

She moved over his reclining body, and he helped her lower herself onto him. Rhea almost cried out as they were exquisitely joined. Completely filled, ecstatic, she rolled her hips sinuously against him. Hux responded by anchoring her firmly with his hands and thrusting upward.

She moaned as the room—or was it the jungle?—started moving around her. The lush-green walls became a leafy backdrop for Rhea, the mysterious dancer unabashedly and lovingly pleasuring her man.

Her hips slowly undulating in the age-old, instinctive rhythm, she heard Hux gasp. His caressing hands roamed over her heated flesh, inciting her even more. She threw her head back, her hair grazing her back.

Lost to sensation, Rhea again visualized herself as the dancer, this time wearing nothing but a necklace and earrings of flashing gems. As she and Hux moved together, the jewels gave off blazing sparks that lighted the blossoming trees and the steamy pools around them. It was growing hotter.

There was a fire burning in the jungle, flaring, blazing, leaping from leaf to leaf, skittering across the waters, to lick at her with molten tongues of flame. Golds, oranges, every shade of red whirled around her as Rhea called out Hux's name.

The escalating spiral of need inside her climbed toward explosion. They whirled together, immersed in a conflagration that deepened into dark reds, blues, and finally absolute white. At the topmost ecstatic point, Hux's body rapidly coming into hers again and again, Rhea cried out with him . . . and fell. Floating, spiraling downward like a burning cinder on the wind, she came to rest . . . on the floor of the jungle . . . back home . . . safe in her lover's arms.

Later, when she awoke, everything was dark and quiet except for the sound of a light, rhythmic tapping on the window. It sounded like sleet, Rhea thought dreamily. She focused her gaze on the window and saw large wet flakes turning into rivulets.

Stretching and turning over, she reached out to touch Hux's body, but felt only the cool of bedsheets.

When had they gotten into bed? she wondered groggily. Willing her mind to resurface, she remembered making love more than once, the last time leading them to the bedroom. But where was Hux now?

Raising her head to peer across the darkened room, she noted a telltale strip of light beneath the bedroom door. Did Hux always get up and wander around after making love? she wondered, remembering the last time.

Or had he left? Heart thumping, Rhea climbed out of bed to investigate. She found a filmy negligee and put it on. Could he really have left again, and on her birthday?

Opening the door to the softly lit outer room, she immediately saw him in her work area. He was seated at the massive wooden desk, carefully inspecting something on top of it.

She stared. "What are you doing, Hux?"

"Rhea."

Smiling as though nothing were unusual, he quickly stood to stride bare-footed across the rug toward her, dressed in nothing but his briefs.

"I woke up and I was restless, so I came out to look at your art collection. I saw Ngamé's design on your desktop," he told her, "so I stopped to admire it."

She flexed her toes against the cold floor. "I thought you'd gone."

"I wouldn't sneak off and leave you in the middle of the night." She shivered and he took her in his arms. "What's the matter? Are you cold?"

"A little. It's sleeting or snowing outside something awful."

"Come on back to bed and let me keep you warm."

His embrace made Rhea's heart feel warmer too. Hux wasn't leaving, and perhaps he'd stay around for quite a while. Maybe, in spite of their differences, an on-going relationship might eventually be possible. Willing herself to have courage and patience, Rhea realized she'd have to give that relationship a chance.

CHAPTER EIGHT

Trying to arrange her rather damp hair and to apply lipstick in the executive bathroom, Rhea accidentally slashed a streak of iridescent copper across her chin.

"Damn!" she swore softly, quickly swiping at the mistake with a tissue. If anything else were to go wrong this morning, she'd collapse in frustration.

The day had started with Rhea awakening at ten o'clock and realizing she had a meeting at Haldan-Northrop at eleven. Cursing the fact she'd forgotten to set her alarm, she frantically showered and threw on the wool suit she hadn't had time to press.

Then, hurrying out to the street, she caught a ride downtown with a particularly reckless taxi driver whose swerves and bumps made it impossible for her to give her video proposal a final going-over. She managed to arrive at her destination barely on time, only to spill her folder of sketches and proposal pages onto the dirty, icy sidewalk in front of the store.

And it was all Huxley Benton's fault.

Last night, he'd made her forget everything. Still, even as Rhea dealt with the chaos of the morning, she judged the previous evening with him worth it.

In spite of her present, extraneous aggravation, her heart had felt—*now felt*—aglow.

A secret smile curved her lips as she yanked open the door of the ladies room. A startled secretary in the hallway jumped back but Rhea smiled reassuringly and the woman tentatively smiled back. Then, glancing at her watch, Rhea hurried toward the executive conference room. It was five past eleven. Would the vice-presidents hold a few minutes of tardiness against her? She knew some people were amazingly neurotic when it came to punctuality. Feeling her shoulders stiffen with tension, she tried to remember something pleasant to relax her.

Unbidden, images of Hux came to mind. She remembered how he'd appeared when saying goodbye at about seven that morning. Hair slightly disheveled, eyes tired but loving, he'd kissed her tenderly and promised to see her that very evening.

After he left, she'd turned over to go back to sleep and awakened much too late. Oh, well, it wouldn't help to worry about it now.

Composing her face into what she hoped was a professional expression, Rhea opened the conference-room door to find a group of seven people waiting for her. Hux sat at one end of the long table, scrubbed and neatly turned out as usual. He gave her a meaningful look that was quickly shuttered when June Sterling spoke.

"Good morning, Rhea!" the vice-president exclaimed brightly. "Take a seat. We're all looking forward to this."

Pulling out a chair opposite Hux, Rhea greeted another woman and four men as June introduced

136

them. It all went so quickly, Rhea couldn't remember exactly which name went with which face, but she took pains to smile and meet each individual eye to eye as he spoke. Although she thought her video concept could win on its own merits, it wouldn't hurt to be personable.

"So, what's the plan for this meeting?" asked Bob O'Rourke, vice-president of credit and financing.

"I'll allow the lady to go first," offered Hux. "Rhea can present her idea."

"No, that's okay," Rhea objected, trying to be generous. The weekend with Hux had made her feel like granting him favors. Besides, presenting second would give her a few minutes to rearrange the notes and sketches she'd spilled. "You can start," she insisted.

Accepting her offer graciously, Hux rose to set a couple of rough drawings on an easel. Giving them a cursory glance, Rhea furtively opened the folder in her lap and started to sort.

"So the best theme for the video comes from the title of the boutique and consulting service itself—revealing 'the hidden woman'," he began. "The models will be dressed as cleaning ladies. They can be working around the boutique's floor and then we'll cut to where they're cleaning a display window. Their clothes are drab, the world outside looks drab . . ."

Hearing only parts of Hux's speech as she dealt with her own pile of papers, Rhea paused at a particular design of Ngamé's. An Arab-like robe with a dark veil, it was the same outfit she'd imagined on herself as a dancer in her erotic fantasy the night before. Grinning as she gave herself credit for re-hearsing her proposal in some way, Rhea quickly placed the sketch at the front of her folder and turned her attention back to Hux.

". . . Then with the wand they find, the cleaning ladies conjure up a fantastic apparition. I think a sparkling dress and crown would do, something that will make this person look magical, like a fairy god-mother."

Rhea pricked up her ears. What was Hux saying about a magical conjuration?

"Here's a sketch of the costume for the god-mother," Hux said, pointing at the illustration on the easel, "and one that shows you roughly what the cast of cleaning women would wear. Of course, by magic, just like Cinderellas, they're all transformed by the fairy godmother. The models cast off their cleaning rags to reveal glamorous or professional clothing—new designs available at The Hidden Woman."

As she realized what Hux was suggesting, Rhea's mind began to whirl. His idea was incredibly similar to hers! She'd planned to dress models in somber Arabic robes and have them find a magic lamp whose genie would zap them into new outfits. How was she going to explain her proposal's similarity when it was her turn?

"After their transformation the women dance or strut through the store to the music on the sound-track."

Dancing? What was going on? Rhea knew she hadn't talked about her idea to Hux. She hadn't said a word about her women dancing around after they'd been changed by magic.

"Eventually the former cleaning women go back to the display window where they were working before. Outside they see a new, colorful world. Lovers and admirers await them, political campaigns, mountains to climb . . . whatever they choose. Because the women have been transformed, their view of the world has been transformed too."

Already upset, Rhea stiffened at Hux's last words. Why, they were almost identical to the ones she'd intended to say at the end of her presentation!

While listening to Hux field questions from the board, Rhea tried to come up with an explanation for this unpleasant situation. Surely Hux couldn't have read her mind! Then, with a sudden sinking feeling, she realized he hadn't had to. He'd had all the information he needed laid out before him in black and white—in the neatly typed pages on her desk!

Hadn't she found him sitting at her desk last night, supposedly admiring one of Ngamé's sketches? The drawings had been right on top of Rhea's video proposal. How did she know he hadn't lifted the sketches to find her notes underneath? Was Hux that competitive? Heart pounding erratically, she wondered if he would stoop so low in order to win. Surely he wouldn't steal her idea and be outrageous enough to offer it almost word for word to the board.

"About how many models do you think the project will require?" asked June.

"Have you done a cost analysis yet, Hux?" asked Bob O'Rourke.

"I like your work, Hux," said Milton Newbold, the chairman of the board. "You're a man of many talents

139

which will be appreciated on an even broader basis by Haldan-Northrop in the future."

Hux grinned widely at that remark.

Taking note of his pleased expression, Rhea remembered Hux had said he wanted to rise within the ranks. He'd said he would do anything to become a vice-president, and this coup could be another stepping stone toward his goal. But Rhea would never have suspected Hux could go to such lengths—spending a weekend making love to her just to get at her papers. No wonder he'd gotten up two different nights to search her apartment. She'd interrupted his furtive task the first time, so he'd had to try again! Hadn't she known his interest in her was too good to be true right from the start?

Ignoring a strong inclination to break down and cry, Rhea instead willed herself to be calm and unemotional. She hoped no one would think her expression strange. When Hux glanced at her curiously, she quickly looked away so she wouldn't gaze into those lying green eyes.

Feeling numb but determined, Rhea rose to present her proposal when called on. Holding her folder in tightly clenched hands, she spoke almost automatically, pausing only to remove and display Ngamé's sketches at appropriate times. The vice-presidents listened politely and, for the most part, silently. There were only a few murmurs when Rhea mentioned the magical lamp, the genie with transformative powers, and the changed world at the video's conclusion. No one reacted negatively to the similarity between her concept and Hux's.

In fact, when Rhea was finished, June seemed

pleased. "I was sure you two would make a great team." June looked from Rhea to Hux. "Even your ideas mesh."

"But I prefer the cleaning-women costumes. They're more contemporary," said Bob O'Rourke.

"And cleaning women won't offend any political or ethnic groups," remarked the other woman board member. "There's a large population of people from the Middle East in New York."

"And Americans don't like to be reminded of the highway robbery Arabs are getting away with for their oil," said Milton Newbold.

Seething inside, Rhea nevertheless remained silent as the board discussed the two ideas for a few minutes. She was not surprised when they quickly and unanimously decided to use Hux's concept.

"We mean no slight to you of course," Milton told Rhea. "Since your ideas are so alike, you can work on the project with Hux as if the concept were your own."

It was close to being her own, all right, Rhea thought angrily. How could Hux sit there and have the nerve to looked pleased! Did he think she wouldn't care?

"So Hux and Rhea are to be co-producers of the video," said June. "Well, this situation is certainly working out agreeably."

Feeling distinctly disagreeable, Rhea wished she could bolt for the door. As soon as she could politely take leave, she rose and hurried down the hall to grab her coat. Then she almost sprinted for the elevators, stabbing angrily at the down button. She was about

141

to repeat the action when a large tanned hand covered her own.

"Where are you going in such a hurry, darling?" Hux's smooth voice assaulted her ears. "Are you starving to death? I was planning on taking you out to lunch."

She turned to face him. "Why? So I can watch you gloat over your victory?"

"What? Are you angry over the board's decision?" He looked surprised. "Surely you're not as competitive as all that, are you?"

"At the moment I'm outraged!" she cried. Then, as an office worker ambled past and stared, she lowered her voice. "You have no ethics in any area of life, do you, Mr. Smooth Talker? Did you actually think I'd be so besotted by your charms that I wouldn't know where you got your video concept?"

"What are you talking about?" He frowned.

"It seems you don't even have enough values to admit it, Hux, but I know you stole my ideas!" As he leaned closer, Rhea backed away.

"Have you gone crazy? Why would I want to steal your ideas?" he asked incredulously. "I have plenty of my own. And if they're similar, it's probably because we think alike."

"Oh, sure. Your idea for the end of the video is almost word for word 'similar' to mine. I'm sure you'll say you only accidentally peeked at the proposal I left on my desk last night. But I know you saw it beneath Ngamé's sketches. I even caught you at the task."

"I didn't notice anything but the design. I was look-

ing around your apartment to see if I could get an idea for a special belated birthday gift for you."

Caustically, Rhea said, "I thought *you* were my special birthday present."

"I wanted to get you something to look at when I'm not around."

"You're never going to be around again as far as I'm concerned. You're one of the most unprincipled men I've ever known! Not that I think my opinion will stop you from carrying on as usual. I'm sure your fabulous proposal will help you obtain that vice-presidency you said you'd do anything to get."

"I didn't mean I'd do anything unprincipled," he said defensively.

Glancing away from him when the elevator door opened, Rhea moved aside for two people getting off. When she tried to enter herself, Hux grabbed her arm.

"Let go of me!" she hissed.

"We're not finished discussing this," he said stubbornly, his face turning red. "Come back to my office and I'll close the door."

"I'm not going anywhere with you after the way you've misused me. Do you always have to be on top, no matter what the competition . . . or the price you make others pay?"

"You're raving!" he exclaimed angrily. "I wouldn't misuse you to get a better position. I can't believe you have such a poor opinion of me after all . . ."

"I should have known better than to trust you," she told him, "and with your background, what else could I expect? You care for nothing but yourself and what you want. We're simply from the opposite ends of the universe."

Dashing quickly inside the empty elevator, she heard him call her name as the doors shut. By the time she reached the main floor, tears were streaming from her eyes. Did Hux really not care that he'd broken her heart?

For Rhea knew clearly now that she loved him. She had to admit it. She was tired of ignoring her feelings or pretending they were something else. Although she'd tried to fight her attraction to Hux from the beginning, the man had gotten to her.

Leaving the store for the gray day outside, Rhea wondered how she could have fallen in love with a shallow, unethical playboy. Where was her usual common sense?

But then there'd always been a unique aura about Hux. And eventually he'd been convincing enough to make her think he was sincere. Furthermore, Rhea wasn't the only one who'd been falsely impressed. Her family had liked Hux and her sweet old grandfather, who'd never said a word to any of her boyfriends before, had asked the man about his intentions. Thinking about that, Rhea felt a new blast of wrath that dried her tears. She'd brought home a con artist! The whole Mitchell family had been fooled!

But then, Rhea decided, her family was simply open and kindly toward everyone, and Hux was charming. She now understood that he made a profession of hiding his competitive, scheming self under a heavy coat of gloss. Such skill had brought him far and would undoubtedly take him further professionally. Rhea was certain Hux would receive the store vice-presidency he wanted so badly.

And she hoped he'd choke on it.

A few weeks after the disastrous meeting with the board, Huxley Benton strode into Haldan-Northrop in the worst possible mood. So far this morning he'd awakened late, hadn't had time for breakfast or even coffee, had groggily pulled on navy socks when he was wearing a brown suit, had lost three taxis to elderly women, and had found himself walking to his place of business in the midst of a freezing drizzle.

If that weren't bad enough, he had an overbooked day ahead of him, Hux remembered, straightening the damp coat collar he'd pulled up around his neck to protect himself from the icy wetness.

"Hey, Benton, I want to talk to you about the new brochure you let Irene design to promote our food services."

"Ah, Glover," Hux said, warily eyeing the old complainer. "Come up to my office in ten minutes, all right?"

"You got it. Several things have to be changed," the older man went on, even as Hux stepped into an elevator.

Hux knew he'd have to deal with Glover quickly. Then he had a conference with the cosmetics staff, lunch with the one department head who dreamed up the worst, most impossible promotion ideas, followed by an interview with the board about the opening for the vice-presidency. More meetings would follow, including a business dinner.

Then, to really make his night, the shoot on the

fashion video for The Hidden Woman would resume after the store had closed. He didn't have time to think about the situation with Rhea Mitchell now, Hux decided as he alighted from the elevator on the executive floor.

It was going to be a killer of a day.

His day got even worse the moment his secretary spotted him. "You already have three messages. All from Sam Monroe."

"Get him on the line, would you?" Hux mumbled, entering his inner office. If the director of the fashion video had called three times . . .

"Rhea's trying to make more changes!" Sam Monroe bellowed into Hux's ear as soon as the call got through.

"God, what now?"

"She wants the fairy godmother to float over the cleaning women as they're transformed."

"What's wrong with that? Last night we agreed on shots that would give us the illusion . . ."

"Forget illusions. She wants the real thing. Harness, piano wires, and all. Do you know how much time it'll take to set up that kind of thing, not to mention what it'll cost you?"

"We can't afford expensive special effects. That lighting change the other night took a big bite out of the budget," Hux grumbled, thinking remorsefully of the film wasted and of the costly models standing around watching the crew reset the lights.

He remembered how Rhea had become displeased with the lighting only after they'd been shooting for three hours. And no sooner had he been fool enough to accede to her wishes when he could swear he'd heard her whisper cheerily, *"Just testing!"*

"We'll go ahead with the shoot tonight as planned."

"Thank God. I wasn't sure you'd be reasonable about it."

If only Rhea Mitchell would be reasonable, Hux thought, returning the receiver to its cradle. If only she hadn't jumped to the wrong conclusion . . .

Why couldn't she believe they'd developed similar ideas because they thought alike? He'd thought of the idea for the video when Melissa had told him about her job telling fairy tales. And his ending—though duplicating hers—had come from within him, inspired by Rhea. After all, Rhea had made him believe that if he could change, his world would change too. Applying that philosophy to the video concept had merely been one more step in a logical progression.

Of course, Rhea hadn't seen it that way, and she'd done her damnedest to make his life miserable the past few weeks, starting by insisting the video be shot totally at night for "a legitimate atmosphere." Since the board had given her equal say in the proceedings —and since he'd hoped they could heal the rift in spite of the way Rhea had mortally wounded him with her misplaced distrust—Hux had foolishly agreed.

And that's when she'd snippily admitted shooting at night would actually be more *convenient* for *her.* The fact that *he* hadn't had enough sleep for a week now would probably please her no end!

Wearily, Hux shook his head, still bewildered by

"I merely made a budget decision," he said sweetly, forcing a smile as they stopped barely a foot apart.

"Really? I thought I was supposed to have some say about *our* project."

"You do."

"But that doesn't include budget decisions?"

"You wouldn't want to use up the remaining money on a single special effect and not have enough left for editing. Or would you?" he asked in challenge.

That took the wind out of her sails! Hux noted with satisfaction. But Rhea still looked decidedly irritated —and so lush and lovely Hux wanted to take her right there!

"I understand all about budgets, Hux. You could have called me and discussed the situation like a rational adult."

"Just as you did when you issued those orders?"

"Now wait a minute!"

"Besides, how could I have discussed it with you? Sam called me early this morning . . . while *you* were still sleeping."

"Oh." Looking slightly uncertain, Rhea did an about-face, rushing back toward the boutique. But Hux was sure he heard her mumble, "Just wait for my next move."

What move? Hux wondered, glaring after Rhea suspiciously. What would she try next?

It wasn't long before he found out.

They completed filming the "magical" scene. As each model whirled for the camera, she was shot in slow motion twice—first in her rags, then in her "hid-

149

den" outfit—with the camera in the same position, the angle unchanged. In editing, the two shots would be blended so the audience could see the transformations taking place.

Now the equipment was being moved around so Sam Monroe could get the wide shot he wanted, with the women dancing toward the cameras—and toward the windows on the changed world outside.

Quiet till then—though Hux was positive he could hear her brain churning—Rhea finally spoke. "I think the fairy godmother should be part of the celebration."

Preparing for battle, Hux folded his arms across his chest. "Really? In what way?"

"By dancing with the others of course."

"That's not the way it was choreographed, Rhea. The other women dance away from her while she looks on benignly."

"Well, the choreography can be changed so the fairy godmother is more involved with her subjects. It's only fair, since she can't fly over their heads."

"Hey, wait a minute!" complained Theresa, the dignified middle-aged woman playing the part. "When I was hired, no one said anything about flying —or dancing."

"We'll pay extra," Rhea assured her.

"I'd love the money," the woman told her with a huge grin, "but I can't dance."

"That settles it." Hux felt so smug he practically hugged himself. "She can't dance, so forget it."

But Rhea ignored him. "That's ridiculous. Everyone knows how to dance *something*."

"Not me," Theresa insisted. "Not even the two-step."

"You can learn."

Hux noticed the woman's eyes grow large with alarm. "Learn? When?"

"Now."

"In case you don't remember, the choreographer isn't here tonight," Hux reminded Rhea. "She's at that opening we insisted she attend since her work here was finished."

"The choreographer isn't the only one who knows how to teach dancing, Mr. Know-it-all Benton. I taught at one of those tacky ballroom dance studios when I was in college."

"You what?"

"I had to pay my way through somehow," she muttered. Thrusting out her jaw, Rhea grabbed the smaller woman's wrist and pulled her away from Hux. "Come on over here. I'll show you some simple movements." Letting go of Theresa, Rhea demonstrated. She swayed, loose-limbed, rotating her hips as she stepped to the left, then changing the direction of her hip movement as she stepped to the right. "See. It's easy. You can do this over and over again. Maybe add some head rolls and hand movements."

"You're putting me on, aren't you?"

"No, of course not. Try it." Rhea moved next to her. "With me."

Theresa tried to imitate Rhea. Hux choked back a laugh so as not to hurt the poor woman's feelings. She moved like a fluffy blue duck having trouble with its waddle. The impromptu performance drew a crowd. The models and crew seemed to have as hard a time

151

as he in keeping a straight face, so it was no wonder Hux's jaw slackened when the woman said, "Hey, that's not so hard."

"Places everyone!" Sam shouted, approaching his crew. "The lights and cameras are ready. I want to rehearse this next shot a few times."

"Wait a minute," Rhea said, still swaying with Theresa in awkward tandem. "We're not ready."

"Who's we?"

"The fairy godmother doesn't know her steps yet."

Sam looked puzzled. "She doesn't dance."

"She does now," Hux told the director dryly, ready to make himself felt. "Rhea, what you've been doing is too complicated for a beginner. If you want her to dance tonight, you'd better let me help."

"You? What qualifies you to teach her?"

"I'm a better dancer than you are," he said, ignoring Rhea's indignant gasp. "Come on, Theresa. Let me simplify that for you."

But as he started to show the middle-aged woman a suggestive hip roll, Rhea grasped him by the upper arm. "I was showing her what to do!"

"Thanks for warming her up for me." Hux turned back to Theresa who was edging away from both of them. "Now, as I was saying, you'll do much better if you follow my . . ."

"You just can't stand it, can you?"

Rhea's wrath-filled challenge made Hux turn and look directly into her eyes. They were blazing like miniature twin volcanoes and he had the strangest urge to hide from the impending eruption. "Can't stand what?"

"Not being recognized as the best. Not having the

152

final word." She was ticking off her points on her fingers. "Not having everything your way, when you want it! You don't care about anyone else."

"Uh, Rhea," Sam said, putting a placating hand on her arm and uneasily glancing at the restless cast and crew. "Can you hold on to those profound thoughts until *after* we finish this shoot?"

Unceremoniously shoving the director out of the way so he could get closer to the infuriating woman, Hux demanded to know, "Are you trying to imply I'm self-centered?"

"That's about the nicest word I can think of to describe you at the moment!"

Even hearing Sam's loud groan and curse, knowing the situation was getting way out of hand, Hux couldn't stop himself. He and Rhea were so close he itched to reach out and take her in his arms. Instead, he began to rant.

"You are the blindest, most incredibly frustrating woman I've ever had the misfortune to meet, Rhea Mitchell! Where's that intuition you women are supposed to be famous for? Maybe if you had any—"

"So now you're saying I'm not woman enough for you?" she cried, coming even closer. "That's certainly a boring cliché. Where's the famous Benton wit?"

"You've made me lose my sense of humor."

"Good Lord, what's going on?" a crisp feminine voice interrupted Hux and Rhea, who stood nose to nose. "I could hear you on the next floor."

"Oh, June! How nice to see you," Hux said as though the vice-president hadn't stepped into the

153

midst of a full-scale battle. "Stop by to see how things are going?"

"Actually, I was working late and on my way out when I heard the commotion. Can I speak to you two?"

With one last glare at each other, Hux and Rhea meekly followed the vice-president away from the set.

"We were having a creative discussion," Hux told her.

"Yes, well, from what I understand, the two of you are driving the director crazy with your impossible demands and constant changes," June said.

"I assure you, I'm innocent of those charges." Hux spoke righteously, yet shriveled slightly under June's knowing gaze. Well, perhaps he had added to the problem—but Rhea had started it!

"I don't know what's going on between the two of you, but I suspect there's more to it than creative differences." The vice-president sighed and for a second was a woman rather than an executive. She looked at Rhea sympathetically, but there was iron in her tone. "And whatever it is, it has to stop, at least while you're representing Haldan-Northrop."

Rhea spoke first. "I am sorry, June."

"So am I."

"I realize you both want to be here while the video is being filmed, but I'd appreciate it if you'd stay away from Sam Monroe. You're giving your director an ulcer."

With that, June was off toward the elevator and Hux was left feeling a little foolish and a lot let down. "Truce?" he suggested softly.

154

"Truce."

Hux followed Rhea back to the edge of the set and they watched the proceedings in silence. Would they ever talk and laugh normally again? What could he do to convince Rhea he hadn't slept with her to steal her ideas?

His belated birthday gift—Hux had almost forgotten! He really had been trying to decide what to buy her when she'd found him at her desk. . . .

He'd discovered the necklace the next morning, shortly before the fateful board meeting. The artist had called the museum-piece look-alike a "necklace of paradise." How appropriate, especially since a small carved goddess hung from the collar of copper and semiprecious stones. Unfortunately, it hadn't been for sale or Hux would have had proof of his innocence to nullify Rhea's accusations. He'd had to commission a duplicate that was supposed to arrive in the mail any day.

Or maybe Rhea had already received it, Hux thought dispiritedly, and the belated birthday gift didn't make any difference to her.

Maybe, in spite of their physical attraction, Rhea wanted him to be guilty because she didn't think he was good enough for her. Was that why she was always pointing out her superior life-style and background? Though he always tried to deny it, Hux had always known there was something missing from his life—something he now was sure Rhea could give him.

If he turned to her right this minute and told her

she'd made him want to change his world, would she believe him? Would it make a difference?

But Hux had learned to live with loneliness long ago and he knew he could never tell Rhea that particular truth.

CHAPTER NINE

Rhea scanned the faces around her as she pushed through the crush of guests attending Haldan-Northrop's gala party in celebration of the upcoming opening of The Hidden Woman boutique. Where was Grandpa Boviak? she wondered. Several hundred people had previewed the new fashion video, watching cleaning ladies transformed into beautiful women on the television monitors positioned around the boutique area. But she could not find her grandfather in the crowd.

As she moved through the throng of people, Rhea was pleased to overhear many positive comments about the video's use of special effects and its mesh of fairy tale and fashion. She was going to talk to people about it in depth, and help herself to the buffet of champagne and hors d'oeuvres—as soon as she found Grandpa.

Where on earth could he be? Since he'd told her sister Diana he was going to the men's room more than an hour ago, Rhea had checked that place first. Then she'd circled the perimeters of the floor's large, roped-off party section, searching the formally dressed throng for an elderly man dressed in an ancient blue suit that was a little too large for him.

But so far she hadn't spotted him. Rhea was a little concerned. Although she knew Grandpa was feisty and independent, preferring to take care of himself, she also knew his arthritis sometimes made it difficult for him to walk very far.

She'd been surprised when he insisted of coming to the party in the first place, especially as her parents had to stay in Queens for a special event at their church. But she had already agreed to bring twenty other relatives and friends to ensure her own fun at the celebration, so she couldn't very well refuse Grandpa. Fun wasn't the only reason she'd invited so many either. Being with a group made it easier to avoid Hux.

In the past few days, since receiving his belated birthday present in the mail, she'd been mulling over the situation quite a lot. Could she have made a mistake in calling Hux a thief? Perhaps he'd been telling the truth when he said he'd been looking for a gift idea in her apartment.

Once again feeling guilty over the stunts she'd pulled during the production of the video, Rhea frowned. Then she shook her head to clear it. She didn't want to think about her relationship with Hux tonight.

Smiling at Bob O'Rourke and another board member as she passed them, Rhea managed to squeeze her way through a cluster of socialites who were arguing about the value of buying New York versus Parisian designers. On the other side of the cluster she almost ran into a broad, well-tailored back. Glancing up, she recognized Hux's blond head.

Damn! Afraid he'd turn and see her, Rhea started to edge away. But she needn't have worried. His full attention was directed toward an attractive reporter from a women's magazine.

"The video is a great promotional idea, Hux," said the reporter. "I'm impressed with your originality."

"Thanks, but I can't take all the credit," said Hux. "My co-producer, Rhea Mitchell, and I both came up with the idea."

"Is that so?" The woman scratched some notes on the pad she was holding.

"Rhea's very talented. Uncovering women's hidden beauty—the basic concept behind her fashion consultation service—was the inspiration for our video. And both Rhea and I envisioned the women's physical transformation affecting their outlook on the world."

"How interesting." The reporter scribbled some more.

Rhea was amazed at what she was hearing. Contrary to her expectations, Hux was actually sharing the credit instead of taking it all for himself. She couldn't resist breaking into the conversation.

"Good evening, Hux."

"Well, Rhea! Speak of a creative force and she appears," he said with a big grin. When his green eyes moved over her, she wanted to squirm. Instead, she smiled nervously.

"Hux is quite a creative force himself," Rhea told the reporter.

The woman laughed. "My, my. You two are a regular mutual admiration society. No wonder the video turned out so well. I'll put a blurb about your success in the spotlight section of *Style*. Can I call you both at the store?"

When the reporter left, Rhea gazed at Hux sheepishly. "I've been wanting to thank you for the gift you sent me. The necklace is beautiful."

"I thought it would do you justice."

"I should have worn it tonight."

He stepped closer. "You should be with me tonight."

Rhea took a step away. "But we have a lot of things to talk about . . ."

Her words were interrupted by the noisy approach of a slender young brunette. Wearing a lot of makeup and a backless, pencil-slim red dress, the woman handed Hux a glass of champagne and cooed, "Here, Huxie! Now we can get really bubbly!"

"Um . . ." Looking extremely uncomfortable, Hux searched for words. Finally he said, "Uh, Rhea, this is Lorraine. She works in the store's cosmetics department."

"Hux is advising me about modeling," Lorraine enthused, possessively grasping his arm and leaning against him. "And he's going to show me all the important places to be seen in town!"

"How entertaining," said Rhea politely. A sudden chill swept through her. How dare Hux flirt with her when he already had a date! "It's nice to have met you," Rhea told Lorraine, "but I must be going." Turning her back on the couple, she walked away as swiftly as she could.

"Rhea!"

Refusing to turn at his call, Rhea wandered blindly into the crowd. It wasn't as if she hadn't expected Hux to revert to his old ways. It was just that she hadn't been ready for the full impact of seeing him with someone else—or for the pain she would feel. And she hadn't missed the fact that Hux's new someone was probably an ultrafashionable size eight.

Emotions churning, Rhea berated herself for ignoring her better judgment and getting involved with the wrong man. Because even if it turned out Hux was more scrupulous than she'd thought, even if he hadn't stolen her video idea, he was still from a totally different crowd. They could never be together. A handsome, elegant playboy from Manhattan and a plump pudding from Queens would hardly make a match.

Plump pudding?

Wait a minute! What was the matter with her? She hadn't felt this insecure about her appearance since high school! No one should ever make her feel this way about herself. When she spotted Ngamé at the champagne table, she headed directly for the designer, hoping a few friendly words would help her to a better mood.

Unfortunately, Ngamé was already engaged in a question-and-answer session with a couple of media people. "The collar and armbands I'm wearing were strung with beads from my ancient ancestors' tombs," Ngamé said, indicating the elaborate jewelry she wore with her flowing white dress. "I was born in Egypt but I came to this country as a little girl."

"Your ancestors were pharaohs?" asked one of the reporters.

161

"No, but I'm descended from royalty."

Rhea hung back. So much for talking to Ngamé. She only hoped the reporters hadn't already heard a contradictory story from the designer during another interview.

Walking away, Rhea knew she should be spending more time this evening talking to the media about her consultation service. That's just what she'd be doing right now if she hadn't gotten into such a funk about Hux and, before that, if she hadn't been busy searching for her missing Grandpa. . . .

Suddenly remembering her interrupted quest, Rhea swung around slowly, gazing all around her. She noted, at one end of the floor, the performance platform where the musicians were setting up their amplifiers and microphones.

Skirting the buffet tables, Rhea determinedly made her way toward the small stage. She recognized José Tiendas, the popular Latin singer, who'd been contracted to perform a medley of classic love songs for the celebration. Giving some last minute directions to his piano and bass accompanists, José paused as Rhea came toward him.

"Can I do something for you, lovely lady?" he asked with a charming smile.

"Can you make an announcement? I've lost my eighty-two-year-old grandfather." Rhea pointed to his microphone.

"Really? How sad!" responded José sympathetically. "But he will sing with the angels now."

"No, no. You misunderstand," said Rhea. "He's not with the angels. He's lost—out there in the crowd.

162

Would you ask him to meet me here? His name is Edgar Boviak."

"I'm so happy he lives. And I'll do anything for a pretty woman." José flashed his white teeth in a flirtatious grin. Then ordering the sound technician to turn up his microphone, he announced, "Edgar Boviak. Please come to the stage. Your beautiful granddaughter is waiting for you. Edgar Boviak."

But Grandpa didn't appear. Getting worried after ten minutes, Rhea stared around the room. José's remark about angels had given her the creeps. Feeling distracted as she hurried to find her sister, Rhea hardly noticed a tiny blonde trying to keep pace with her.

"Hi! Rhea Mitchell?" said the blonde, taking two strides for every one of Rhea's. "I'm Melissa Damon —a friend of Huxley Benton's."

"Excuse me?" Rhea slowed down.

"I've been looking for you tonight. I've wanted to meet you for a long time."

Looking down curiously—Melissa barely reached her shoulder—Rhea recognized the pregnant fairy she'd seen in Hux's office a few months ago. The tiny woman's condition was even more apparent now, although the rose-colored, Empire-waisted dress she wore was quite flattering.

"Please excuse me for being abrupt," Rhea said, extending her hand. Gazing down into the blonde's sincere blue eyes, she was struck by how they looked both innocent and wise. "It's nice to meet you, Melissa, and I'd like to talk. But can we do it a little later? Right now I have to find my grandfather. He seems to be missing."

"Can I help? I can search in one direction while you go in another."

Touched by Melissa's kind offer, Rhea told her, "Well, if you'd like, we can search together. My relatives won't be happy until we find him." As they strolled along slowly then, Rhea admitted, "I'm a little worried about Grandpa myself, although I'm sure he's all right. He's probably talking to someone."

"Your grandfather came to see your video tonight? How nice!" exclaimed Melissa in silvery tones. "I've heard so much about your family—and *you*—from Hux."

"You have?"

Melissa nodded. "Hux has been friends with my husband Rafe since college. He visits us a lot. He's even agreed to be our baby's godfather."

"Really? That should be a new experience for him."

"I'm sure he'll enjoy it. My two stepchildren adore him already. Hux is such a lovely person—generous, loyal, caring. He just hides those traits beneath a cynical facade. But I'm sure you, of all people, know that. In your profession, don't you delve beneath the surface, look for the hidden beauty in a person?"

Though Melissa's expression was innocent, Rhea thought her tone made the question significant. "I try to do that."

"Rafe and I think you're a good influence on Hux. He needs people who believe in his inner self, who expect good things from him. Hux has had too much experience with those who don't believe in anything. He wants to change his life."

"Did he actually say that?" asked Rhea. Why was

164

this sweet little woman going out of her way to bear witness to Hux's good character? Did she really know him that well?

"Rhea!" called Diana, rushing up to her sister, with Aunt Augusta following behind. "Look! There's Grandpa near the buffet tables. I called to him and he waved his cane at me to stay away! How do you like that?"

"I told you he was all right," Rhea said with a sigh of relief. Staring toward the buffet, however, she stiffened when she saw Grandpa Boviak about to accost Hux.

"Oh, Lord, no," Rhea moaned. "Diana, didn't you tell Grandpa that I'm no longer seeing Huxley Benton?"

"Yes, I told him."

"Well, why is he hanging around the man then? It could be very embarrassing for me. Hux brought a . . . new girl friend to this party. What am I going to do?"

Diana shrugged. "Don't ask me. If Grandpa wants to run after Huxley, I guess we can't stop him. Our grandfather appears to be acting very strangely, if you ask me."

Looking at Rhea, Melissa said, "But sometimes appearances can be deceiving."

Having introduced gabby Lorraine to a leading cosmetologist, Hux was sipping champagne and enjoying the comparative quiet when he saw Grandpa Boviak heading toward him. For a moment Hux froze, his hand with the glass stopping on the way to his mouth.

165

He could hardly believe his eyes. Had Rhea actually brought her grandfather tonight? Then Hux smiled, partly from amusement at the incongruity of Grandpa hobbling along in the middle of the posh gathering and partly from delight at seeing the old man again.

"Grandpa Boviak!" Hux exclaimed, holding his other hand out for a shake. But Grandpa didn't return the gesture. Instead, he brandished his cane. "Are you planning to beat me with that?" asked Hux. "I really don't deserve it, you know."

"Hmmph. I doubt if I could beat you," said Grandpa, puffing a little as he lowered the cane to lean on it. "I'd have to catch you first and that's not easy. Why, I've spent the better part of this evening trying to run you down. First, you get on the elevator and go up to the top floor. Then, you're gone by the time I get there."

"Sorry. I didn't know you were here—or wanted to see me."

"And then, after that," Grandpa continued, pulling out a large white handkerchief to mop the perspiration from his forehead, "I got off on the wrong floor and wandered through all those tables piled up with women's dainty-looking underthings. Why does that stuff cost so much? It can't be very warm."

"Sounds like you've had a wild time," remarked Hux, raising his eyebrows. "Would you like to sit down and rest?"

"What? I'm not helpless," objected the old man, scowling fiercely. "Don't start treating me like I'm ready to die. I'm a healthy eighty-two." He shook his cane again. "And I'm still ready and able to represent

166

my family. That's why I came to this shindig tonight. What did you do to my granddaughter? She hasn't been happy."

Hux laughed nervously and took a deep swig of champagne. "I didn't do anything, Grandpa Boviak. I'm afraid there's been an unfortunate misunderstanding."

"Who misunderstood who? Does it have anything to do with that skinny girl you've been running around with tonight? You said you had honorable intentions toward Rhea."

"Lorraine is just a fellow employee," explained Hux. "Honest, I'm not interested in her. I still want to see Rhea. She just doesn't want to see me."

"You mean she got mad at you?"

"Yes, over something I didn't do."

"And you didn't try to explain?"

"She doesn't believe me."

Grandpa narrowed his eyes. "You give up real easy. I gave you credit for having a little more backbone. Are you sure there's not more to this?"

Hux cleared his throat. "Uh, Rhea may also be put off a little by my, uh—my background."

"Your family? You mean she disapproves of them? Are you from the wrong side of the tracks then?" Grandpa ran his eyes over Hux's elegant clothing—a well-cut tuxedo and pleated shirt set off by a gray satin bow tie and matching cummerbund. "Well, you're doing a good job at working your way up, son. Rhea should appreciate that and she's always been able to see good things in everybody. Don't worry about your family." The old man paused, and then

167

said, "There's only one important thing I have to know."

"What's that?"

"Do you love Rhea?"

"Uh . . . yes." Hux answered Grandpa's inquiry with some embarrassment.

"Have you told her?"

"Not yet."

Grandpa poked him in the ribs with his cane, making Hux jump in reflex. "Well, that's what's wrong then. Women always have to be told you love them. I'd of thought a good-looking boy like you would know that. Go and tell her you love her right now. That'll make all the difference."

"You think so?" Hux was indecisive.

"Tell her," admonished Grandpa. "I saw the way you two were mooning over each other at Rhea's birthday party. Why, I never saw that girl so nervous about a boyfriend before. And you hardly noticed anybody but her. That's why I asked you about your intentions. You two reminded me of the days when I was young and courting—and fighting—with Helen, my late wife."

"Does Rhea love me?"

"I expect so. Ask her. Go and talk to her right away. Don't waste any time. Take it from me—life is too short."

But after Grandpa left him, knowing he had to clear up the current situation, Hux went to look for Lorraine rather than Rhea. He told Lorraine the truth—well, a close version of it anyway.

The ambitious young woman looked only mildly

168

surprised when Hux told her he wasn't really a
swinging playboy, that he wanted to settle down. But
Hux was certain she was positively appalled when he
continued, saying he wanted to buy a house in the
dullest section of New Jersey and get a station wagon
for the dozen kids he hoped to have. After that pro-
nouncement, she readily agreed that they had different goals and assured Hux he wouldn't have to see
her home. There were a lot of other interesting men
at the party anyway.

And now, striding across the floor in search of
Rhea, he realized his fibs had their basis in reality. He
really did want to settle down, though he didn't actually want to move to New Jersey. Did he have
enough nerve to tell Rhea that truth?

In spite of Grandpa's remarks, Hux had his doubts
about Rhea taking him back. Besides accusing him of
being a thief, she'd said some pretty nasty things
about his life-style and background. He'd seen the
way she glared at him when she saw him with Lorraine tonight.

Hoping against hope to win Rhea back anyway,
Hux stepped up his pace, trying to avoid the other
guests as he sped along. He stopped short when finally he caught sight of her on the dance floor. Gulp-
ing down a lump in his throat, Hux watched Rhea
move slowly and provocatively to the soft rhythm of
a love song—while wrapped in another man's arms.
He quickly changed his position to get a view of the
man's face. When he saw Rhea's partner was Jerry
Hastings, the man with the problematic suit, he felt
oddly relieved. Hadn't Rhea said she and Jerry were

just friends? That's probably why they weren't dancing very close.

Buoying up his courage, Hux strode across the floor to tap Jerry on the shoulder. "Can I cut in?" he demanded. His tone must have been insistent because Jerry stopped in midstep, released his partner, and backed away without a word.

Looking confused, Rhea held back. "Haven't you already got a partner, Hux? What happened to your girl friend?"

"Girl friend? Lorraine isn't my girl friend." Slipping his arms around her and drawing her tightly against him, Hux was reassured by Rhea's quick intake of breath. "Lorraine's just a fellow employee looking for a promotion. And don't worry, she's going home with someone else."

"I'm not worrying. So someone else is going to show her the best places to be seen?"

"Right. I don't know who exactly, but she'll find somebody. She's very aggressive. I ought to know, since she invited herself along with me tonight."

"Literally forced herself on you, huh?"

Mesmerized by the moist full lips so close to his own, fascinated by the soft peach-toned skin, breathing in the subtle fragrance of her perfume, Hux said assuringly, "Lorraine wasn't . . . isn't any competition for you, Rhea. She isn't half the woman you are."

The tilted amber eyes bore directly into his. "You mean she's half my size, don't you?"

Suddenly aware of her insecurity, Hux was surprised. Running his fingers lightly over the sparkling surface of her gold-shot pink evening sweater, he said with feeling, "I meant nothing of the sort. You really don't know how beautiful you are, do you?"

"Maybe I can't distill the truth from your smooth lines."

"To love, one has to trust."

"Do you want me to love?" Her exotic eyes seemed lit with golden fires.

"Um . . . I want us to try and work things out," he said, feeling edgy. In spite of Grandpa's suggestion, he simply couldn't bring himself to tell her exactly how he felt—yet. Instead, he nestled her more deeply into his arms, his lips grazing her cheek. As they circled the floor slowly, he moved one hand lower, bringing her pelvis into intimate rhythm with his own. She took a deep, shuddering breath.

"I think we can work things out between us if we have a chance to talk," Hux murmured silkily into her ear before giving the lobe a tiny nip.

"Talk?" Rhea croaked as though she didn't understand. She stirred restlessly in his arms, her movements arousing him further.

"Yeah, you know, put one word after the other," Hux said, gratified at the way he could distract the woman he loved. "As in discuss all the things that bother us. Clear up our misunderstandings."

"Oh. Okay." Tilting her head back, she wet her full lips, making Hux long to kiss them. Intent on doing just that, he lowered his mouth, only to be stopped by a question. "So when are we going to have this important talk?" she asked.

Rhea was agreeing! he thought foggily, and muttered, "How about tonight . . . I mean, tomorrow?"

"Tomorrow?" Her brow drew in to a frown and Hux panicked. Was she changing her mind?

"Let's have dinner tomorrow," he insisted quickly, telling himself that would surely allow her enough time. At the moment he wanted only to take her home and ravish her, but he would have to be patient.

Rhea's frown deepened. "But tomorrow's Easter, Hux. I have to go to my parents' house. Aren't you having a family dinner?"

A holiday! And Rhea always shared celebrations with her family even as she had tonight. His sore ribs where Grandpa Boviak had poked him attested to that. "That's what I meant, Rhea," Hux said, without considering the consequences of what he was saying. "I want you to join my family for Easter dinner."

"Well, all right. I'll go. I'm sure my family wouldn't miss me for one holiday."

Even as she said the words, Rhea was surprised at her own eagerness. After all the trouble she'd had with the man, she'd gone ahead and accepted his invitation anyway. Rhea knew she'd be sorely tempted if he asked her to go home with him tonight. But she was determined to resist.

At this point, talk was more important than making love. If they wanted a relationship, they needed to straighten things out between them. And hadn't Hux hinted at a deeper commitment when he mentioned love and trust tonight? Could he love her half as much as she already loved him?

CHAPTER TEN

What had he done? Hux wondered later. He'd invited Rhea to have dinner with his family. Had he lost his senses? Well, he was clearheaded enough now to realize how badly he'd goofed. But just how was he supposed to pull this one off?

As usual, his sister Charlene would spend Easter with her husband's family—in-laws she could barely tolerate, or so she'd always told him. As for his parents, Hux wasn't even sure they were in town. If the elder Bentons were at their Long Island estate and did agree to the idea of a family dinner, they would no doubt find some way to spoil the afternoon. If they didn't cancel at the last moment.

Why had he been so impulsive? And how could he admit his mistake to Rhea now without seeming like a fool—or the liar and cheat she already thought him to be?

Hux hadn't remembered Sunday was a holiday until Rhea had mentioned it, but aware of how important these special family gatherings were to her, he'd meant to impress the woman he loved. He desperately wanted to be important to her too.

So he'd lied.

Somehow he'd make sure *this* Easter dinner came off! Hux decided, still amazed Rhea had actually accepted. Suddenly energized by what that might mean in terms of her feelings for him, Hux had a brilliant idea.

Maybe he could *rent* a family—hire some actors. Clarence, who'd played Santa and the Easter bunny, had legitimate theatrical experience. Well-spoken, the old actor would make a perfect father. And then there was Clarence's friend Terry, one of the Christmas elves. He could be Hux's brother. Did Rhea know he didn't have any brothers? Hux thought feverishly but couldn't remember discussing his family at all except for that time he'd tried to win her sympathy. But just to be safe, he'd better introduce Terry as his cousin.

But who could he hire to play his mother and his sister? What if he couldn't find anyone, Easter being a holiday and all? Contrary to his own experience, Hux knew just about everyone else made family plans on major holidays, and he was sure actors were no exception. He'd have to hire people without families then.

Suddenly Hux imagined his Easter disaster: He'd been forced to hire nonactors from the soup kitchens of the Lower East Side. And instead of praising their beloved Hux to Rhea as he'd most definitely instructed them to do, they were too busy filling their stomachs with the culinary delights spread before them—and stuffing their pockets with his silverware.

Well, there went the rented family ploy. Hux guessed Rhea would never have gone for it anyway. She was too intelligent to be fooled so easily. Besides,

174

he couldn't keep his real family from her forever. More's the pity.

What in the world was happening to him, the man who had put up yellow and purple lights that spelled "Bah, Humbug!" during the Christmas season? Who displayed the British flag on the Fourth of July? Why was he so determined to have this holiday gathering? Was he really so love-crazed that he'd consider doing *anything* to win Rhea's heart?

Honest with himself, Hux knew there was almost nothing he'd stop at . . . not even blackmail.

Recalling a slightly lurid incident from his sister's college days—one he'd helped her cover up and that she would never want her snobby friends or their mother to find out about—Hux grinned broadly.

Charlene had once posed nude for her photography-major boyfriend. At eighteen, she thought it a lark—until the guy told her he was going to sell the photos, that is. Hux had come to his sister's rescue, first finding and burning the photos and negatives, then blackening both of the creep's eyes. He could threaten to tell all. Not that he'd ever actually go through with it, of course—deliberately hurting someone was out of the question—but his sister wouldn't know that.

First he'd invite Charlene nicely, but if he couldn't convince his sister that her dear, love-besotted brother desperately needed her help . . .

Well, then, Hux would let Charlene think he was ready to join the ranks of master criminals to see that Easter dinner came off!

175

*   *   *

"Don't you think we ought to start dinner, Huxley, dear?" Charlene asked, taking a drag on her cigarette. "That's the purpose of this little get-together, isn't it?"

"Yeah, I'm hungry, Uncle Huxley!" his three-year-old niece added, leaning forward to peek at the stuffed toy rabbit in the center of the formal dining-room table.

"Chloris!" Charlene had only to use the child's name to make her sit back and to subdue the sparkle in her excited blue eyes. "Behave yourself. I could have left you with your nanny even if Uncle Hux did insist you be here."

"Let the child be," Charlene's husband Daniel Hancock mumbled as if by rote, not even bothering to look up from the business section of the Sunday newspaper. "Chloris can't help it if she's hungry."

"Uh, let's give Aunt Priscilla another five minutes to get here. All right?" Hux asked anxiously.

He gave Rhea a reassuring smile, but Rhea was far from being reassured.

This was a family holiday celebration? she thought with wonder.

"But, Huxley, dear, Aunt Madeleine and Uncle Norris have already cancelled, so Aunt Priscilla probably means to do the same. I'm sure she's just forgotten to call. You know the poor dear is going senile. Why, she can't remember her own name half the time." There was definite disapproval in her voice as Hux's elegantly dressed sister added, "I don't know why you invited her in the first place."

"Because even if she is half-dotty, she's family,"

176

Hux said politely, but Rhea felt him tense beside her. "I think it's time we all remembered that."

Charlene merely rolled her eyes and took another drag on her cigarette in answer. Hux moved closer to Rhea on their love seat.

Opposite them, three little robots with hands folded neatly in their laps sat wedged between their parents on another uncomfortable-looking couch. In addition to Chloris, there was six-year-old Baxter and eight-year-old Amanda. All were decked out in their finest—and had obviously been prewarned not to wrinkle a garment.

Was it the uncomfortable atmosphere Charlene had created the moment she walked in the door and rebuffed her brother's embrace—or the expensive, too perfectly furnished house—that kept the children unnaturally quiet?

Or had they actually taken that old maxim—"Children are to be seen and not heard"—to heart? Only little Chloris seemed to defy the rules of the adult game, at least to the extent of wiggling her patent-leather Mary Janes occasionally, cocking her head from side to side to see her reflection in them.

The phone rang and Hux jumped to answer it. "Hello?" His tone was hopeful, but his lips tensed as he listened. "I'm very sorry to hear your lumbago is acting up again, Aunt Priscilla." Obviously the old woman then went into some detail, for Hux listened a long while, nodding as though in agreement. Finally he said, "Well, we'll get together some other time then. I hope you feel better soon. Happy Easter."

Trying to dispel the awkward silence as Hux slowly

lowered the receiver, Rhea asked, "What time did your parents say they'd be here?"

Hux seemed acutely embarrassed and looked away from her to his sister. "They didn't. They told us not to wait dinner for them if they, uh—were detained."

"Why didn't you say so in the first place?" Charlene tossed back her long, pale-blond hair and stubbed out her cigarette in an art-noveau ashtray. Then she rose gracefully, brushing invisible wrinkles from her silk designer dress. The children followed her example like small automatons. Would they march to the table in step? Rhea wondered as Hux's sister signaled the butler. "Jerome, we'll be sitting down to dinner now. Daniel?"

The thin man dutifully followed his vociferous wife to the table set for twelve people. And there were only seven of them, Rhea thought, glancing at Hux who was slightly behind her. His growing unhappiness was evident. Distressed for him, Rhea furtively took his hand and squeezed it reassuringly. He seemed to brighten a bit, until his sister made disparaging remarks about his wasted effort.

"You should have known it would turn out like this, Huxley. I don't know why you bothered to put on this big show."

Was Hux actually turning red? Rhea pretended not to notice and allowed him to seat her. If Hux should have known his relatives would cancel, why in the world had he gone to all this trouble? It didn't make any more sense than holding the dinner at his parents' Long Island estate when they'd planned to be away for part of the day.

Rhea looked down the long table at the crooked

stuffed Easter bunny which served as centerpiece, incongruous with the pristine linen, sparkling crystal goblets, fine china, and polished silver. There was something about the toy that touched her deeply. Perhaps because it was another example of the warm heart she'd always known Hux had since that day she'd seen him fuss over the pregnant fairy at the store. The stuffed animal would appeal to children, and she was sure it had been placed in the midst of all that elegance by Hux.

Rhea realized she wasn't the only one curious about Hux's unusual centerpiece. Ensconced in an overstuffed chair next to her, little Chloris sneaked furtive looks at the stuffed animal whenever she thought her mother wouldn't notice.

"Jerome, what is this?" Charlene asked as the butler brought in a huge platter.

"I do believe it's called a turkey, madam."

"I know what it's called! But why has it been prepared?"

"One would dare to guess . . . for your consumption?"

Rhea smothered a grin at the butler's sarcasm. It was obvious Charlene annoyed him as much as she did everyone else.

"Huxley, dear, didn't you check the menu before the chef prepared the meal? Turkey. How very unoriginal. And boring. I haven't had turkey since my senior year in college when I stayed in the sorority house for the entire Thanksgiving holiday," Charlene told him without a trace of nostalgia. "Why didn't you have Marcel prepare Thai food or Cajun? Blackened redfish is very popular, you know."

"Yuk, I hate fish," Baxter mumbled, earning a glare from his mother.

"The turkey was my idea, Charlene," Hux told her stiffly. "I thought the children would enjoy it."

Amanda finally spoke. "I like turkey, Uncle Huxley."

"Me too!" yelled three-year-old Chloris, who promptly picked up her china plate to stare at her reflection.

"Pardon me, madam, but my arms have grown fragile since those days when you two were children," Jerome said dryly. "May I set the turkey down and carve it, or shall I return the platter to the kitchen and tell Chef Marcel his bird has displeased you?"

"No, don't do that," Charlene said with a bored sigh. "I don't want to spoil my day further by arguing with Mother's servants. If Marcel were to quit, she'd never let me hear the end of it."

Dinner was a strained affair, conversation practically nonexistent, as though brother and sister hardly knew each other. Adding in his parents' absence, Rhea got a great deal of insight into Hux's familial relationships. Remembering the incident in the bar when Hux had told her about his loneliness—and how later, to her fury, he swore he'd made it all up—Rhea now suspected he had been telling the truth in the first place.

Was Charlene a replica of her mother? Was Jerome the butler who'd "savagely" forced Hux into the limo that had taken him away to boarding school? Rhea smiled at the image, even knowing Hux's youthful

180

perception of the incident hadn't allowed for amusement.

She hoped Charlene's children would have better memories of their youth when they became adults. They were in the midst of eating apple pie and ice cream for dessert when Chloris pointed and asked her uncle, "Where'd you get the rabbit?"

Before Charlene could interrupt, Hux answered. "Actually, the Easter bunny himself left it."

Chloris's blue eyes grew large. "Really?"

"And he left Easter eggs and all kinds of candy hidden around here as well. He said that whoever found the most eggs could have the stuffed rabbit as a prize."

"Can I look now?" Chloris eagerly asked, then sobered under her mother's disapproval. She dropped her spoon into her dessert dish. "I'm not hungry anymore."

"Where have you gotten these antiquated ideas, Huxley?" Charlene asked.

"I thought it would be fun," Hux said halfheartedly. "What do you say, kids?"

Amanda and Baxter looked at each other, then at their mother's set frown. Rhea noticed the repressed eagerness on their faces. Though she hadn't said anything, Rhea had earlier noticed several colors staining Hux's fingers as he'd lifted his water goblet. So he'd gone through the trouble of coloring Easter eggs for Charlene and Daniel's children, and they didn't even care!

"I don't know about anyone else," Rhea said loudly, rising and giving the kids an encouraging smile, "but I'm going to hunt for those Easter eggs."

Amanda, Baxter, and Chloris looked hopeful.

Daniel cleared his throat and gruffly muttered, "I might like to join in the hunt if one of you could show me how. What about it?"

"I'll help you, Daddy," Chloris said, struggling down from her chair.

In moments the staid, expensively furnished Benton living room had turned into a noisy playground with Rhea and Daniel doing a cursory search, letting the children find most of the eggs and eat all the candy. Hux declared himself the scorekeeper and collected the brightly colored Easter eggs one at a time.

"You're not very good at this, are you?" Amanda asked Rhea. Behind a chair the girl had found an egg the woman had purposely overlooked.

"I guess it's been a while," Rhea admitted.

"Yeah, besides, you're way too big." Startled that Amanda could be so rude, Rhea merely stared. But it seemed the child hadn't meant anything negative, because she added, "Grown-ups can't crawl into the small spaces kids can, so we have the advantage." After thinking about it a second, she thrust out her hand. "Here, you can have this one."

Rhea felt like smiling at the girl's generosity, but forced her mouth into a serious line and shook her head. "If I win, I want to think it's because I did it on my own."

"Okay then."

Amanda ran over to Hux to give him the egg. He smiled at Rhea. She winked in return and continued her casual search.

Amazingly, none of the priceless collectibles dis-

182

played on every uncovered surface were broken, although there were a few close calls. Chloris almost knocked over a Lalique glass bowl as she whipped by it. Catching the spinning bowl, Rhea found that, unbelievably enough, Hux had used it as a hiding spot. She tilted the expensive receptacle and an egg rolled into her hand.

"How am I doing?" she asked, handing it to Hux.

"Terrific," he whispered. "You're way behind."

And in the end, even Charlene gave in and joined the search long enough to find one egg, giving it to a delighted Chloris.

"I count thirty-six eggs here," Hux declared as the little girl turned it over to him. "That's the whole three dozen the Easter bunny left." He counted the three collections, skipping the few eggs the adults had found. "Let's see. Amanda has eight. Chloris has nine. And Baxter has ten."

"Yea! I won!" the boy said, jumping into the air. He collected his prize from the table. "Isn't he neat?" But when he turned and saw—as Rhea already had—that Chloris was looking away, her blue eyes filled with tears, his smile of victory faded. Without hesitation, he offered the stuffed rabbit to his little sister. "Here, Chloris, you can keep him for me. But you gotta let me play with him too."

Rhea thought she'd never forget the heartwarming picture the two of them made, both trying to hold on to the crooked bunny and hug each other at the same time. Touched by the boy's generosity, remembering how Amanda had offered to give up one of her eggs, Rhea decided Charlene's kids would indeed have some good memories in future years—at least of each other.

What a disaster, Hux thought during the ride back to Manhattan. Rhea had sat next to him in silence ever since they'd left his parents' estate. What was she thinking? Though the sun was just now setting, he couldn't see her features because she kept turning away from him. Hux wouldn't blame Rhea if she were thoroughly disgusted with him after the fiasco he'd just put her through. He was disgusted with himself, wasn't he?

He'd done everything wrong, starting with blackmailing Charlene into bringing her family to dinner. His sister probably wouldn't be civil to him for the next several years, even if he assured her he'd never seriously think of revealing her secret.

But it wasn't Charlene he was worried about. It was Rhea. Hux felt her slipping further and further away from him with each succeeding mile. She'd said their backgrounds and life-styles were too different to mesh and he'd just proved her correct, hadn't he? Depression closed around him like an airless coffin, choking the life out of him. Rhea had been his last chance for a future filled with happiness and love, it seemed. He'd gambled like a desperate man—and lost.

Why couldn't he have been straightforward and honest for once instead of playing a lousy game? The answer was simple: He'd been afraid of rejection.

Rhea stared out at the cars on the highway, wondering why Hux was so silent. Foolish question. He'd gone to so much trouble to have a terrific family holiday dinner and his sister had systematically undermined him, completely ignoring Rhea in the process. And his parents had never even bothered to call to say they wouldn't be there. What kind of family did he have anyway? Rhea was indignant on his behalf once more.

Therefore, when he said, "Uh, I'd like to apologize for the disastrous dinner I invited you to, Rhea," she was properly irate.

"There's no need for apologies, Hux. What happened wasn't your fault."

"Really?" Hux took his eyes off the road just long enough for the Porsche to swerve a little too close to another car. He quickly regained control. Rhea closed her eyes and took a deep breath in relief. "Sorry," he muttered.

"Stop apologizing."

Turning to him, Rhea scrutinized the man hiding behind the three-hundred-dollar gold-framed Gucci sunglasses. Hiding. That was it. She'd finally come face to face with the truth.

The playboy who wore thousand-dollar suits, handmade Italian shoes, and sunglasses to match his car wasn't the real Huxley Benton any more than the competitive show-off she'd wrongly accused of stealing her ideas. Those were merely his facades. Always having prided herself on being a good judge of character—having founded her business on revealing the hidden beauty in a person—Rhea couldn't figure out why had it taken her so long to find the hidden man in Hux.

His outrageous behavior was a plea for attention, something he obviously lacked in his family life. He'd

185

developed himself into a man who would be noticed and admired, certainly not a man who could be easily overlooked. But she'd seen glimpses of the real man underneath and had done her best to ignore him. Why?

"I can't help feeling bad, Rhea," Hux went on. "It was stupid of me to think I could pull off a pleasant dinner, but I had to try."

"I don't understand. Why?"

"To prove I was worthy of you."

To say she was stunned would have been an understatement. "You were trying to prove yourself worthy by inviting me to dinner?"

"I know how important family is to you. When you assumed I'd spend Easter with mine as any normal person would, I wanted you to think my background was no different from anyone else's. But I made a mistake, and I'm sorry about ruining your holiday."

"My holiday is doing fine, thank you very much. But I do think we have a lot of things to discuss if we're ever going to develop this relationship," Rhea said with the certainty of a woman who'd finally been convinced her man was serious about her.

And with that realization came another, more important one about herself—the reason why she'd ignored Hux's hidden nature so studiously. She'd manufactured reasons to convince herself their relationship wouldn't work—from telling herself their backgrounds and life-styles were incompatible to accusing him of stealing her ideas. But all the time it was just that she'd doubted a man like Hux could really want her, a woman who wasn't acceptably thin. Though Rhea had been sure she'd come to terms with her weight long ago, she now realized she hadn't been as secure as she'd thought in withdrawing from the battle of the bulge.

Hux's words suddenly cut through her thoughts. "You still want to talk about us? Not tell me to get lost?" His amazement was evident.

"I have no intention of letting you get away, Huxley Benton," Rhea told him, realizing they were back in Manhattan. "But I'd like to get to know the real you a whole lot better. Isn't that why we're together today? You're the one who said you wanted for us to talk, so why don't we go to your place?" she suggested, anxious to be alone with the man so she could make it all up to him. "You've never invited me there."

"Only because we've spent more time making war than love lately," Hux said, his tone teasing and intimate.

"That situation is easy enough to correct," Rhea murmured, placing her hand intimately on his thigh.

With that incentive, Hux made it to his place in record time, taking corners like a true New York cabbie. At his elegant high rise he cursed as he fumbled with the card that opened the overhead door of the garage. Those mumbled words were about all he uttered until he'd whisked her into his apartment on the thirty-third floor.

"Let me take your coat."

Rhea gave Hux a melting smile. "As long as you don't intend to stop there."

He practically ripped the coat off her before she had both feet in the door.

Hux's apartment came as no surprise to Rhea. It

was a marvelous example of expensive Eurostyle, from the dove-gray leather couches and chairs to the gun-metal macroblinds covering the floor-to-ceiling windows. The gigantic living area was a study in perfectly co-ordinated monochrome, with only a few touches of color enlivening it.

Hux even matched his surroundings in his burgundy-and-gray Armani sweater and gray-wool trousers, Rhea noticed as they settled themselves comfortably on one of the leather couches. She wondered if he'd planned it that way.

"So let's talk," she said, suddenly realizing Hux's green eyes were glazed with fear.

"I, uh, wanted you to know how I felt," he croaked. "Though I'm sure you already know anyway."

Was he referring to her woman's intuition? Rhea wondered, remembering he'd intimated such a thing once before. "How exactly *do* you feel?"

"I, uh . . . I guess I love you," Hux said in an embarrassed rush.

"But you're not sure?"

"Of course I'm sure! I've loved you since . . . since Ngamé's party."

Rhea blinked in surprise. He'd known all that time, but hadn't told her? "Why didn't you say so?" she demanded indignantly even as her heartbeat quickened with happiness.

"Because you never let me!"

"I never let you? What a thing to say! You're the one who was always trying to trick me—"

Hux cut off her heated accusation with a simple question. "Do you love me?"

Looking into his jungle-green eyes, Rhea was mesmerized by what she saw in them. Love. "Yes, of course I do."

"Then why didn't you tell me?"

"What happened to your male intuition?" she asked breathlessly.

"Hmm. You got me there," Hux said, inching closer to her. Rhea pretended not to notice as his fingers brushed lightly over her shoulder. But her body certainly couldn't ignore the exquisite sensation. "Maybe I didn't tell you because you were always pointing out our differences as obstacles. Then I was hurt when you accused me of using you to get a promotion. I was offered the vice-presidency, you know, but I'll turn it down if it'll convince you of my innocence."

Fighting the growing languor spreading insidiously through her, Rhea made her confession. "I already know you didn't steal my ideas. I'm ashamed I made such horrid accusations, but I guess it was my way of protecting myself. You know, my leaving you before you left me." She was unable to admit the reason for her insecurity, however. "You'd really give up the vice-presidency?"

Stroking her face gently with his fingertips, Hux nodded. "If it would make you happy."

"I want you to be happy too." Rhea kept her voice innocent when she added, "If being part of a large, normal family will make you happy, perhaps I could suggest a way . . ."

"You mean marry into it?"

"You want to marry me?" Rhea practically choked on the question.

189

"I thought you'd never ask," Hux murmured, lowering his head to kiss her.

The moment his lips touched hers, she responded with all her heart. Hux loved her and wanted to marry her! Pressed against his chest which seemed to thunder with his heartbeat, Rhea couldn't imagine a place she'd rather be. She slipped a teasing hand down his back and under the waistband of his trousers. His heated flesh warmed her fingertips, but Hux's head popped up instantly and he seared her with blazing eyes.

Breathlessly, he whispered, "I can see our wedding now. A small chapel filled with white roses. Just you and me and a few of our friends. And your family of course."

"Wait a minute," Rhea said, trailing her nails along the flesh just below his waist. She couldn't resist challenging him. "Wouldn't the wedding be more effective in a large church. Something like St. Patrick's?"

Hux took a long, hard look at her, then wiggled away from her fingers. "Don't try to distract me, woman," he said, deciding to play along with her game. This was the old Rhea, the one with whom he'd fallen in love. "I don't want our wedding to be a media event."

"Why not?" Rhea's amber eyes were widely innocent, but she trailed her fingers along a new, more daring path around his waist. Hux sucked in his breath as she insisted, "Publicity would be good for both our careers."

"It would, would it?" And he'd thought they'd never banter and laugh together again. It seemed Rhea would always be a delightful surprise for him.

190

"And what were you thinking of wearing? An Arabic veil over . . ."

"Nothing? Well, perhaps on our wedding night. But for the wedding itself? Tch, tch. Shame on you, you sexy beast."

"Beast? As in lion? I thought I was a snake."

"If I'm a charmer," Rhea said in that sultry voice of hers, slowly dipping her hand lower, "I can change you into anything I want."

Hux effectively trapped her teasing hand between them by throwing himself at her and winding his arms tightly around her body. He finally had Rhea Mitchell exactly where he wanted her, Hux thought happily as he pressed her against the couch. And he meant to keep her there forever. "And what if I want to wear green?"

"As in leaves? You want me to change you into a plant?"

Hux smiled slowly and sexily, grinding his hips into Rhea as he told her, "I wouldn't mind being turned into a ripe fruit if you promise to nibble on me carefully."

"Yum, a peach."

"Rhea Mitchell, you're an insatiable woman!"

"Me? Who was the one who . . . ?"

Hux prevented her from continuing the teasing argument the only way he knew how—with a kiss that promised he'd love her forever.

Now you can reserve June's
Candlelights
<u>before</u> they're published!

♥ You'll have copies set aside for *you*
   the instant they come off press.
♥ You'll save yourself precious shopping
   time by arranging for *home delivery*.
♥ You'll feel proud and efficient about
   organizing a system that *guarantees* delivery.
♥ You'll avoid the disappointment of not
   finding *every* title you want and need.